KING OF PAIN

LORDS OF LAS VEGAS

TAMMY ANDRESEN

Created with Vellum

KING OF PAIN

A billionaire gangster in disguise
A med student with nothing left to lose…

Powerful
Gorgeous
Sexy as sin

I'm on the worst date of my life.

Not even a fancy Vegas restaurant can save this night because my date isn't just a first-class a-hole, he's a sadistic criminal.

Enter Luke Kincaid. Sure, he's bleeding and broken. And yes, he's trouble.

The exact kind of trouble I've taken great pains all my adult life to avoid. But I'm in it now…

So when he offers me a bargain—his protection for my medical expertise—I accept.

He provides the shelter, wrapping me in his strong arms. I give the care.

It feels so right.

And the sizzling-hot passion that ignites between us, seems completely natural too. So I don't even think as I give him first, my virginity, and then my heart.

It's not until after, I realize it's all been a lie.

He is just as dark, just as dangerous as the men who hunt us.

I'm not safe out there, a storm rages, as the forces of Las Vegas wage war.

But pressed to Luke's side, I'm in even more danger. Because he can wreck far more than just my body.

He has the power to ruin my life and break my heart.

DEDICATION

Dedication: This book is dedicated to the fictional character, Dean Winchester, from *Supernatural*. Luke is my ode to you. Cool, gorgeous, never overthinks things, considers himself the least important when, in fact, he is the engine that drives the whole train, and is the exact guy you want by your side in a crisis.

I love you, Dean.

I love you, Luke.

No one tell my husband.

CHAPTER ONE

Luke

The trunk of a fucking car is no place to get my bearings.

Bleeding from a bullet wound doesn't help.

I blow a frustrated breath through my nose, but I don't pound on the lid of the trunk no matter how much I'd like to vent my rage.

It won't help and it will just burn up my energy. This is a moment for control if I'm going to escape.

I should have known this was coming. The shit my family has been in lately...

Just to get this out there, and in case it wasn't clear, I'm not one of the good guys.

The car, a Lambo, and yeah, trunk space is tight in those fuckers, takes the corner at full speed and I crash into the wall.

That fucker Vincent did that on purpose.

Vigo and Vincent Vendetti are the reason I'm stuffed into the trunk of a car with a bullet wound. They are the reason for a lot of my family's problems lately.

I grit my teeth and try to brace myself.

The car takes another corner, but I hear the engine downshift before the clank of a gate fills my ears.

I catalogue the details as the car finally stops. We've been driving for at least thirty minutes putting us well outside of Vegas. I think.

One, two doors open and close before I hear a third and then… the whimpering of another person.

Fuck. That isn't Vigo or Vincent, that's for damned sure. The sound is high and clear like the cries of a woman.

The trunk opens and Vincent hauls me out. It's got to be two in the morning, the darkness thick and inky beyond the ring of the house lights.

Just to my right, a woman kneels on the ground, a curtain of long, dark hair covering her face. But it doesn't hide her shivering, or the pretty dress she wears. What the fuck?

I just get my feet under me when he pushes me to the ground, waving a gun in my face, as he spits out the words, "Here is how it's going to go, you murdering piece of shit."

Now there is the pot calling the kettle black. I'm no saint, but I've never put a woman in a dress like that on her knees. All right, that's actually bullshit. But I haven't done it to hurt her. If she's on her knees, we're both enjoying it.

"You…" he points the gun at the woman, "are going to patch him up. Fortunately for him, and you, we need him alive."

She doesn't say a word.

"To what do I owe this unexpected show of mercy?" I ask, spitting on the ground right at his feet.

Vigo bends down, looking me right in the eyes. "I had the best date tonight. Gorgeous woman with a very interesting piece of real estate right in the heart of Vegas. I hear it's the perfect location to vent an underground tunnel meant to connect several casinos."

Fuck. Of course, I'm here because of the tunnel. And if I were better at my job, we'd already be in the final phase of construction. "You need me alive to date some chick?"

"No, I need you alive so that your family stops chasing permits and starts chasing you instead." He grins right in my face. "And when those permits don't go through, you can sign over the unfinished project to me."

I didn't think Vigo was that smart. He's gotten several details right that I wouldn't have given him credit for. I am the one in charge of the tunnel project, and without me, my family will scramble to close the deal. They never should have left me in charge in the first place.

The only thing I can do now is make this fucked-up situation right. Which means getting the fuck out of here.

The woman next to me has her chin down, little sobs escaping her lips. I can see her bare knees digging into the stone of the drive.

"And you, cutie," Vincent uses the hand not holding the gun to lift her chin and force her gaze to his, "are going to fix him up and then you're going to join me for the rest of the evening. We've got a date to finish."

She whimpers, shrinking as I push up onto my knees. She looks over at me, a quick glance in my direction is all it takes. "No. Please."

Her voice is small and scared, the tone of it skating down my spine. I catch her eyes, and I have the strangest thought. He's not touching her.

I give my head a little shake. Where the fuck did that come from?

Maybe she doesn't notice my gaze, or maybe Vigo and Vincent scare her too much to lift her head again. I'm not sure she's hearing or seeing anything the way she's trembling. But I shift closer, gritting my teeth.

Vigo points a second gun at my temple. "Don't move, asshole."

Vincent gives me the barest glance before he bends down, getting right in her face. "I paid for fucking dinner, you put out."

The Vendetti twins wear matching bad suits, their V-neck T-shirts clearly visible under their open jackets.

Vincent crops his hair short, making his large nose even more prominent, while Vigo wears his longer, slicked back from his face.

They both look like pricks to me, but my cousin, Arabella, once told me they hold a certain appeal. I don't see it.

And my guess is, if this girl ever found Vincent handsome, she doesn't now…

Vigo hauls me to my feet, wrenching my injured arm, as Vincent wraps a hand around the girl's upper arm, half dragging her up and onto her stilettos.

We don't go up the massive front steps, the gaudy McMansion so in keeping with everything else about these two Italian gangsters.

Instead, we're dragged around back. My legs are starting to work again, the cramping from the car receding.

And despite the bullet wound, my muscles twitch to fight. Vigo walks just behind me with a gun to my back. Vincent in front of me as he half drags the woman, her heels wobbling as she tries to keep up.

My eyes survey the large brick wall that encloses the property and sweep back to the iron gate with a guard.

This isn't the moment.

They pull us toward a small guest house on the edge of a massive pool. Vincent goes first, dragging the woman inside, Vigo, with a gun still to my back, shoves me inside next.

"Supplies are in the back. You've got an hour," Vincent snarls before the door closes and locks.

I stare at the door.

What the fuck? They're just leaving us here? I'm still on my feet. "What is that guy on?" I mutter, looking at the woman who has sunk to the floor once again. She's got her arms around her middle, small sobs escaping her lips.

Fuck me. Two crazy fucking twins, a bullet wound, and a hysterical woman I've already half decided I'm taking with me when I go. Could this night get any worse?

"Hey there, love?" I run my hand over the bloody mess of my shoulder.

She doesn't say a word.

"Why do Crazy One and Crazy Two think you can patch me up?"

Fuck me, she whimpers again looking so frightened and so fragile. I'm going to have to calm her down. I do not have time for this.

But also, not leaving a massive blood trail would be helpful. I crouch down. "I'm Luke. Nice to meet you."

Her head lifts. There's only the dimmest light from the glow of the pool just outside, but I see the shine of her dark eyes, the tiny nose, the full lips. She's also got a fair bit of really gorgeous cleavage on display. "Kate." No wonder my first reaction was lust.

And now we're getting somewhere. "Hi, Kate. What brings you here this evening?"

She stares at me like I'm the crazy one. Probably valid. So, I try again. "How did you end up in the Vendettis' car?"

"You know them…" is all she says as she shrinks away, beginning to scoot backwards on the floor.

"Love," I murmur low and gentle. "There is no need…" But I stop as she vehemently shakes her head, sliding back until her back hits the couch.

I sit my ass on the floor too, trying again. "Judging by the dress, you were on a date?"

"I…" she swallows, her voice cracking. "I just wanted a nice dinner. I…"

I'm going to have to negotiate this one very carefully. "Kate," I say even more softly. "I'm going to try and get us out of here. But first, I'm going to need you to look at my shoulder."

She blinks several times, tears still falling down her cheeks. "Don't let him take me into the house."

I jerk my chin in agreement. "I won't." I can't even explain why I'd make a promise like that, but I do. If I'm going to fight though, first I need her to bandage the bullet wound…

She slips off her shoes, setting them carefully to the side before she pushes to her feet.

Her knees are scraped, her arms bruised. But she brushes her hair back from her face and starts toward a closed door.

She opens it, checks what is clearly a closet and then looks in another. Finding the bathroom, she enters.

Thirty seconds later she returns with a decent sized first aid kit. "I'm going to scrub up," she doesn't look at me. "I'll need you to strip all your clothing above the waist."

I try to unbutton my shirt, but my arm just won't lift like that. I hear the water turn on. "Kate." I call her attention back to me, knowing I'm going to need more of her help. I have no idea how I'm going to keep the promise I made when I can't even unbutton my shirt.

She looks back at me. "Before you scrub up, any chance you can…" I gesture to the row of buttons. If I'm going to have any chance of getting us out of here, I'm trying to conserve the arm for when we might really need it.

She lets out a long rush of air. "Right. Yeah."

Padding back over to me, she stops just in front of me. I can actually smell Vincent's shitty cologne on her, but underneath that….

She smells like the ocean and lilies. Floral with a bit salty musk that makes my teeth grind. I breathe deeply as her deft fingers work down my row of buttons.

"You a nurse?" I try again.

With sure hands, she takes the shirt off my wounded shoulder. "I'm in med school," she answers softly. "Just finished my first year."

"Oh yeah, so a real dummy then?"

A faint smile touches her lips before she gasps at the sight of the bulletproof vest I'm sporting. Her hands drop and she takes a giant step back.

"The vest isn't going to hurt you."

"Are you?" she asks, her eyes wary as she assesses me. She's got these gorgeous cheekbones and large brown eyes, fringed with dark lashes. Full lips and a delicate shape to her face. She looks so vulnerable. I want to pull her close.

"No," I answer quietly. "And you're going to have to trust me on that. We don't have much time."

She grimaces, but nods, and then helps me take off the vest too. And last, comes my T-shirt. I can see a rip, the sleeve soaked in blood.

She grabs the hem, her pretty little hands sliding up my skin as she takes the fabric off my good arm first.

It hurts but I ignore the pain, watching her remove the shirt with slow care that hits some note deep inside me. Gentle and beautiful…

The shirt finally comes off and I look down at my shoulder, relief rushing through me. It hurts like hell, but it looks like the vest caught the worst of the bullet.

Kate returns to the sink, washing her hands. She opens the kit, assesses the contents, and washes her hands again, before putting on gloves. "Come sit."

I take one of the two kitchen chairs, as she bends over me and begins to inspect the wound.

I'm less worried now that I've seen the injury, and her cleavage is fucking fantastic. I hold still until she pushes right on the wound and then I suck in a breath.

"I see the bullet in the vest. I think the edge of the metal cut your skin good, and you'll have a lot of bruising, but..."

"I didn't actually get shot."

She shakes her head, that silky hair brushing over her shoulders. Returning to the first-aid kit, she pulls out gauze and tape, and some butterfly stitches, making quick work of the tape job.

But she's still working when the door bangs open again.

It's fucking Vigo.

He stalks in, smirking at me even as Kate ducks behind me. I stand, blocking her from view.

"Think he's going to save you, Kate?" He sneers. "Think again."

Another man comes in behind Vigo. I assume it's Vincent and draw in a deep breath, widening my stance.

But Vigo only smiles wider. Crazier.

"This is my cousin, Guerriero. He's going to keep you both company. He doesn't speak a lot of English so I wouldn't bother begging." Then Vigo spins, saying something in Italian, before the door closes again and the lock clicks.

The other man glares at me, his eyes hard. His bulging muscles, I'm not going to lie, flex impressively. "That's what 'roids will do for you," I say to Kate as I reach back for her hand.

She slips her small silky fingers into mine, pressing to my side.

"Where...you...go?" Guerriero asks, his accent thick.

"Don't worry, Gorilla," I give him a toothy grin that's meant to make me look like the predator I am. "The lady needs to change. We'll

BRB." And then I start toward the small room I see next to the bathroom.

"What you say?"

I don't answer as I go by Guerriero, who pivots to watch us, and I pick up both my shirts as we pass. "If you can't find anything else we can put one of my shirts on you."

"They're soaked in your blood."

I look down at her, one of my brows rising. "Trust me, covering that cleavage is worth a bit of blood."

She gasps, even as I tug her toward the pool changing room.

There isn't much but there is a robe and a set of men's swim trunks. She wraps the terry cloth around her, cinching the belt tight.

I know we've only got a minute. I'm surprised that ape hasn't tried to stop me already.

In the corner, I find a pair of flip flops and toss them to her.

They've got to be three sizes too big as she slips her tiny feet in them but at least they're better than those heels.

"Where you?" Guerriero growls.

Tucked in the back of the changing room, I see another door. Softly opening it, I find another room with several pool supplies. A skimmer, a pole, and a long-ass string likely used for one of the pool covers. It's my lucky fucking day.

That's when I grin. And I probably look like a crazy person too. Because Guerriero and I are about to tangle.

"Kate. Love," I whisper. "I'm going to need you to hide."

CHAPTER TWO

Luke

Kate jolts, her wide eyes meeting mine, and then does exactly what I ask, slipping through the door I just left open.

If the situation were different, her reaction to my command would have me growling in satisfaction.

But I've got a job to do.

The Vendettis are big on muscles, swagger, and bad behavior. They're light on intelligence, though, and that's how we're getting out of here. By outsmarting them.

I'm not the brightest bulb. In fact, in my family, I'm probably the least of everything. But I can outsmart these three bozos.

Not sure when I decided that Kate was coming with me. Maybe it's the way she looks in the semi dark, tending my wounds. Or maybe I knew the second I looked into those big brown eyes. Yeah. I think it might have been then. So scared. So fragile…

I don't normally get sentimental about the ladies, but her hands feel like silk and every part of her is pretty, from her pinky finger to her slender shoulders, right down to her gorgeous little feet and sweet toes.

So yeah. First, I'm going to have to get Guerriero out of the way. Then, when Vincent comes for Kate…

It's about as good a plan as I can come up with.

And honestly, it's not half bad. It would be better if I wasn't injured. Vincent and Vigo are massive, but Guerriero…

That guy looks like the fucking Hulk.

Jumping up on the bench right by the door, I wait as Guerriero calls again, lets out a rumble and starts stomping toward the changing room. Looks like the Hulk, moves like a rhino.

I wait until he appears in the door and then I bring the pool skimmer pole down right on his head.

It's not that thick and the fucking thing bends around his skull as he roars, taking a swipe and sending me flying across the room. I hit the other wall hard, the pain shooting through me.

Okay. Maybe my plan sucked.

But I'm committed now. I've still got the skimmer pole in my hand, and I make a quick jab, getting him right in the solar plexus.

He doubles over and I don't hesitate, thrusting the pole between his legs and right up into his ball sack.

Fucker goes down like a brick house.

Using the string, I hogtie that Hulk, wrapping him tight. Then, grabbing a dirty towel, I stuff that shit in his mouth. "Love," I call to Kate. "I'm going to need some of that tape."

"Why?" she pokes her head in. "Oh. Be right back."

Her flip flops clip-clap across the house and she returns with a roll of medical tape and small set of scissors.

I take the roll and wrap it several times around his head to hold the towel in place.

He must be recovering because now his eyes are promising death as he glares back up at me while I tape.

"Sorry, Gorilla," I pat him on the shoulder. "But I don't fancy staying."

Then I rise, pulling Kate into the other room. "Listen, love, when Vincent returns it's the same drill."

"We could just leave now."

I try the knob. "Locked. We could break a window, but I don't know if it's alarmed or not."

She nods, nipping at her lip. "I'm just worried about you."

"Thanks, love. But I'll be fine, and Vincent is the ticket out because he should have the keys..."

She nods, squeezing my hand. "Good idea."

"We have two choices once we're out the door. Head to the gate or go over the wall. The gate is risky, the wall difficult."

"The wall," she answers, squaring her shoulders.

"You sure?"

"I do my share of Pilates. I got this."

I wink at her. "Good girl." I test my shoulder. It hurts like a mother. "Are there any pain killers in that first-aid kit?"

"Ibuprofen."

"I was hoping for something stronger," I mutter as she gets out the little packets of pills and opens two of them.

Crossing to the sink, she fills a glass of water, bringing it back to me.

"You know," I say, popping the pills in my mouth and raising the glass to my lips to swallow them down, "you never told me your specialty."

"It's too early to commit, but I'm thinking of becoming a surgeon," she answers.

I give her a one-sided grin. "Beauty, brains, and talent?"

A ghost of a smile touches her lips. "I was out on a date with Vincent Vendetti. You tell me how smart that makes me?"

"Did you mumble something about a dinner?"

She sighs. "Being in school for as long as I have makes a girl poor. He offered to take me out to Volturno and I'd read an article about how great it was, but really pricey."

A sound outside catches my attention. It's only been forty-five minutes but I'm sure Vincent has decided to collect his date early. He doesn't strike me as the patient type.

I wave for Kate to go hide and she thinks to slip off those flip flops before she races into the bathroom, closing the door behind her. I position myself against the wall next to the front door.

I maybe should have traded out weapons. A bent pool skimmer stick wasn't even good the first time.

The door swings open and Vincent strolls in, swaying on his feet. Fucker is wasted.

He doesn't even notice me as he stumbles in. "G?"

"Busy," I rumble before I bring the stick around, smacking the crazy piece of shit with all I've got right in the face…

He shot me two hours ago. I don't feel bad as he falls to the floor. I just wish I had more string.

But crossing to the medical kit, I pull out the three remaining rolls of tape and go to work. Then I grab the keys from Vincent that are hanging out of his pocket.

"Love."

Kate appears a moment later, her eyes wide as she looks at Vincent. "You're really good at that."

"We all have our skills." The fact that this is mine doesn't say much about me. But I gesture for her to come as I grab a kitchen chair from the table.

We slip out onto the pool deck and around the back of the pool house. The wall has got to be seven feet high but with the chair, I'm able to hoist Kate up on the top without much issue. When it comes to pulling myself up, my shoulder hurts like fucking hell, but I get there.

We're straddling the wall facing each other. The robe is tight around her waist but the long length of her legs are on full display, the flip flops in her hand, her bare feet dangling in the breeze.

"I'll jump down and then I'll catch you," I tell her, swinging my leg over one side.

"Are you sure? I know I said your arm was just a cut, but it must hurt terribly…"

I chuck her chin. "I'll be fine, love. Men like me are supposed to break for women like you."

Her eyes go wide, her lips parting in a way that looks completely kissable.

"Let's get out of here and then we can worry about recovery."

She nods, and taking a deep breath, I make the leap. On a normal day, it's not that far, but the landing makes my teeth rattle, pain radiating through me.

Ignoring it, I turn back and gesture for her to jump. She does, landing in my arms.

It fucking hurts like hell, but also, she feels amazing pressed to my body like that. Her arms come around my neck, her breath fanning my face.

I lightly set her on her feet. With one arm still around my neck, she tugs on the flip flops with the other. And then, taking her hand, we're off down the street. "You got a phone?"

"No," she shakes her head. "Vincent took it."

"Mine too," I huff. No calling my family then. They're going to notice I'm gone. Roman too. But I need to tell them what the Vendettis have planned.

And I need to tell them that I messed up the permits. They should have never given the job to me. I can't be trusted with shit like that.

I nearly fucked this whole thing up and it's my job to fix it. Which means telling them the permits have almost expired.

Only Roman knew and last I saw him, he wasn't moving. Roman is ten times smarter than me. I should be on the ground, and he should be here.

Not that I even know where I am. And honestly, directions are not my thing.

But as we slip through the dark, the flip flops clopping along, I see a little Honda Fit parked on the street.

Reaching for the handle, I give it a pull and find that it's unlocked. "Score."

"Are we..." Kate sucks in a breath. "Stealing a car?"

"Think of it as borrowing," I tell her.

"We can't do that."

"You want to keep walking? Vigo's going to come after us when he finds Vincent and Gorilla."

She nips at her lip, and it's cute as shit, a second before she nods.

I get into the driver's seat and pull out the wires, the car firing up as she slides into the passenger seat, closing the door and doing up her buckle.

A laugh ripples from my chest. "Safety first," I rumble before I slam the car into gear and drive off.

She looks over at me, her mouth opening and closing. "You should put yours on too."

"My shoulder is not up for buckling." I could. But it's not worth the pain.

"Oh," she says softly before she unclicks her own and leans over me, her face close to mine again.

Damn, this woman smells so good. Her hair tickles my neck as she reaches in front of me and pulls on the belt, clicking it in place. Then she slides back in her seat and does her own. "Thank you for not leaving me," she says as we start driving through the dark.

"You're welcome," I grunt in return. And then I draw in a deep breath.

Because our night is just beginning, and we've got several things to discuss.

"You any good with directions?" They are like a bunch of things that when they get in my head, I swear they jumble all around. I couldn't navigate for us even if I knew what town we were in. I know we drove for a solid half hour outside of Vegas.

"I'm all right with them but I've only been in Vegas like three days. I have no idea where anything is."

In the rearview mirror I see the headlights of a car go speeding past a cross street, the outlines of a GT3 unmistakable.

"Fuck," I mutter and kill the lights of the Fit, taking a left turn and then hitting the gas. "Good thing you did up those belts."

"What? Why?" she asks, her hand coming to grip my arm.

I hit the accelerator.

It doesn't matter which direction we go this exact moment, as long as we slip away from here. I'll figure out how to reach my family after I know we're safe.

CHAPTER THREE

KATE

I'M GOING TO HELL.

It's not because I'm speeding through the night with the headlights off, while my date and his deranged brother chase us.

It's because...

I think I might be turning into my mother.

The woman is a bum magnet. Like every guy that a woman should not want, she brought home. Tried to pass off as my daddy for the week or month he'd stick around.

I've been so careful to avoid that trap. I don't date. I keep my head down. But now...

This guy has every part of me humming. And I think for the first time in my life, I might understand why she liked bad boys.

I can't even remember this guy's name.

I think he told me, but I was barely paying attention. In my defense, I was still recovering from having a gun to my head.

What have I learned? I know for sure this guy is a criminal. The kind who gets shot, knows how to beat other guys up, really big guys.

The kind who knows how to steal cars…

Man, I know how to pick 'em.

"Can I…" I start. "Can I ask your name again?"

"Luke." He must have the gas pedal pressed to the floor as we take a right turn, speeding through the night.

Luke. It's a perfect name for this guy. Watching him drive, I can feel liquid fire in my panties. It doesn't help that he's incredibly hot. Like way too hot for me.

And the fact that he went out of his way to bring me with him, doesn't help either. Would it be weird if I slept with him?

It would be. It definitely would. The silent lecture going on in my head is epic. I should be worried about why he just killed the lights and hit the gas.

Instead, I picture introducing Luke to my med school friends…

How'd you two meet?

He rescued me after my date kidnapped me. Couldn't control myself after that.

This is not exactly a meet cute line that you tell your friends over drinks.

I could probably tell my mom. She would one hundred percent get it, which is part of why this crazy attraction is so scary.

This is why I don't date. I've kept my head down, focused on my studies.

It's been working for me.

But I've been bored and lonely for a while, and now I'm in a whole new city where I know no one. When Vincent asked me out, I knew he wasn't relationship material. Not even date material. But I wanted a night I wasn't alone.

He had money and connections, and I figured I'd be all right for one date even if he was a "no good" guy. He was attractive enough, though, and I really did want that dinner.

I know better. I should have just said no when he asked me at that bar. If I'd followed my own rules, I'd be fine right now.

But here I am, with Hot Luke—that's what I'm calling him.

He takes several more turns and then points at a sign. "Does that say it's a highway?"

I squint. Without the headlights reflecting off the sign, it's really hard to read. "I think so?"

"Catch which way we're supposed to go?" he asks.

"No. Sorry." Crap. I'm not helping at all, and this guy has done nothing but help me. I can give him that.

But I've got my contacts in, and my eyes are so dry, I can barely see the signs.

"Well. Luck of the draw I guess," and then he takes a sharp turn onto an on ramp.

The moment we hit the highway, he turns on the headlights and I let out a sigh of relief.

I'm still holding his arm, his really muscular arm, and I can't seem to make my fingers unclench.

"Thanks for patching me up."

"You would have been fine without me, the bleeding had already slowed."

He jerks his chin in acknowledgment.

I glance at the speedometer, noting that we're going about eighty-five and the little Fit is vibrating.

It's not exactly a performance car, not that Luke seems to care. He's still got the accelerator to the floor, his jaw locked as his hands grip the wheel.

Dangerous looks so good on him.

I look down, trying to keep my thoughts clean, but that only brings my gaze to his lap.

His thighs are thick with muscles, and the bulge…

There go my insides, dancing and aching. This is no way for me to lose my virginity. Then again, it's kind of pathetic I haven't already.

But like I said. I've been focused on my studies. And trying to prove to myself, and the rest of the world, I can be something, despite the fucked-up way I grew up.

I unlock my fingers from his arm and slide back into my seat.

"Can you check the glovebox for a map?"

"Sure," I say, but I seriously doubt I'm going to find one. No one keeps maps around anymore.

A sign comes up and I note the town before clicking open the glove box and rifling around the contents. Nothing.

"We don't know where we started," I muse aloud. "Or which direction we're going?"

"Right," he answers, his jaw growing even harder. "All we know is that we're headed... away."

I nod. It's not great to drive blindly into the night but at least I'm not in Vincent's bed right now. And I'm so glad to not be alone. "I... uh... I know I said this already, but honestly, thank you for helping me. For not leaving me. It must have hurt like hell to get me over that wall."

"It was nothing, love." He looks over at me with that cocky, arrogant grin that makes my girl bits actually flutter. Like aching, pulsing need, Kegel-type feelings.

I should hate that smile. I know it's trouble. He has all the markers of a "love 'em and leave 'em" kind of guy, but I'm not sure I care.

Lucky I'm wearing a terrycloth robe. Otherwise, I might have left a puddle on the seat.

I have got to get it together.

I blow out a long breath, reading the next sign.

I don't recognize any of the names.

I'm new to the Las Vegas area, came for an internship with a renowned surgeon for the summer. Not only is the opportunity unparalleled, it's paid. I beat out thousands of candidates and the money will go a long way in helping me live for the next year. But it means I have no sense of the Las Vegas area. No idea where we are or which direction we're going.

Glancing at the clock, I note that it's nearly three-thirty in the morning. I'm used to late nights but my eyes still close for a second as I rest them. "How long until sunrise?"

"Hour and a half maybe?"

I lick my lips, trying to make a decent plan. "Okay. So we can see where the sun comes up and at least know if we're headed toward California or Mississippi."

He rumbles a laugh, and I smile too. "Might be making a trip to Mexico."

"Or Canada. Cooler temps would be nice. I'm not used to the heat."

He chuckles again. "Until then, we keep driving in the same direction? Just put distance between us and them?"

I nod. "I'll keep watching the signs. Maybe I can figure something out. I wish I knew the area better."

"You'll still do better than me. I'm navigationally challenged."

I glance over at him. I like that he told me something he isn't good at. Somehow it makes him seem even stronger that he's not afraid to tell me one thing he doesn't do well. Is that crazy?

I don't know, but I rest my head back, watching the desert slip by. I draw in a breath, the purr of the engine soft and gentle.

"You have a last name, Luke?"

"Kincaid," he answers. Like I said, I haven't been in Las Vegas long but the name rings with a familiarity that I can't put my finger on right now.

"Why did my date shoot you?"

That gets a rumble out of him. "Besides the fact that he's a walking dick?"

I smile at that. Luke isn't wrong. "Besides that."

"We're rivals," he shrugs like that explains everything. "And I'm winning."

"Oh," I reply, because that actually makes sense. Vincent does seem like the type of guy who'd get really aggressive if he were losing. I nearly ask him what they're rivals in, but then I catch myself. Might be better if I don't know.

Like I said, I know I'm with a criminal and my date probably murdered a guy and shot another.

"Who was the man you were with?" I ask. "I know there were two of you."

Luke's face goes deadly serious. "His name is Roman. He's my cousin, but he's the closest thing to a brother I've got."

"I'm sorry," I whisper.

He smiles again but this one isn't genuine, doesn't touch his eyes. "Roman is way smarter than me. He's fine. I'm sure of it." But he can't even fake a smile now and I know he's worried.

"Me too," I whisper and then I do what I know I shouldn't, and I reach out and touch his arm again, running my fingertips over the cotton of his shirt.

He looks down at my fingers, his jaw clenching, his eyes following the path I just traced before he looks back at the road.

We drive in silence, none of the town signs or minor roads giving me any idea where we are or where we're headed.

Finally, the sun begins to rise and it's right in front of us. No mistaking our direction now, we're headed east.

And whichever direction Las Vegas was from where we were when we started, we're far away from the city now.

Luke rubs his eyes. "I haven't seen another car for at least an hour. I don't think we're being followed."

In the light of the day, I can see he's just as gorgeous in the light as he was in the dark, but also, he looks tired.

Fine lines fan out from his eyes. "Need me to drive for a while?"

He adjusts in the seat, sitting forward and pulling a wallet from his back pocket.

"I'm good. But can you see what I've got for cash?" And then he hands me the wallet.

I open it up, his ID right in the front with his cocky smile and his name. Lucas Kincaid.

Well, he was telling the truth about that. Another point in his favor.

Not that I need to keep a tally. As long as he's not a kidnapper or murderer of women, I'll be fine, provided I can keep my libido in check.

After years of suppression, I swear, my body has gone into complete revolt.

I open up the wallet, my brow furrowing. "You carry a lot of cash."

He smiles again. "Yeah. Never know when you might…"

"Need to escape the city?"

"I was thinking more like buy drinks for pretty girls."

"Right," I look down again, sure that he does that kind of thing all the time. Buy drinks for pretty girls. Something to keep in mind.

He scrubs his face, letting out a long breath. "Let's see about getting a hotel. It's going to have to be a roadside dive and even then, I'm going to need to charm whoever is at the desk so that I can pay cash and not drop a card, but I don't want to leave any trail for the Vendettis to find if I can help it."

I'm sure he's right. Hotels want people to pay with plastic for security deposits these days. But I'm also pretty sure Luke will manage to work around that. He exudes that calm devil-may-care charm that I'm guessing works every time.

Tiredness pulls at my own eyes.

I've still got dirt embedded in my knees from when Vincent made me kneel on the ground. A shower would be amazing.

And then…

I shake my head. "Sleep sounds good. I can't think at all."

What comes next? Today is Saturday. My internship starts on Tuesday. I've got to be back in time to start.

How bad is this?

I'll ask, as soon as I've gotten some rest.

CHAPTER FOUR

KATE

LUKE COMES out of the motel office, flashing a grin and waving a key. I wave back from my seat in the car.

We are at a rundown motel, with peeling paint and a sign that's got several bulbs out, not that I'm a stranger to places like this. Like I said, my mom was a bum magnet, and I sincerely mean she dated guys on the edge of death or jail. There were a few good ones, of course. But none of them ever lasted long.

Luke slides in the car and drives around the corner to our room. He hands me the key. "I'll be back in an hour. Lock the door behind me and I'll give one quick knock to let you know it's me."

"Wait. What? Where are you going?" Fear tightens my chest. I don't want to be alone now. Even if three deranged criminals weren't chasing us, I have no idea where I am or how to get back to my life.

"Walmart," he answers.

"I can come with you," I say in a rush, grabbing his arm again. I've got no money, no phone...

His eyes slide down my body. "I'm in blood-stained clothes and I still look more normal than you."

"Oh," my face likely turns seven shades of red, because, yeah, I look like I've been dragged through a sewer. My clothing options are a bathrobe or a tiny dress. I've got dirt-covered knees and bruised arms and at this point, I'm guessing my hair is an actual nest.

And I've been lusting after a guy while in a ratty used bathrobe and men's flip flops. Pathetic. "Right." He winks, taking my fingers in his and gently removing them from his arm. "You can get away with a lot of fashion faux pas at Walmart but…"

"Yeah," I take a breath. "I could wait in the car."

"Kate," he starts. "I'm going to leave the car in the Walmart parking lot and walk back."

"But," I furrow my brow. "How will we leave town?"

"That is a problem for when we wake up. What I don't want is for a stolen car to lead anyone straight to our motel room."

I nod. That makes sense.

"So, I go in and wait for you?"

"Feel free to take a shower, close your eyes."

I nod, a shower sounds amazing. But I still don't get out of the car. "Are you leaving me here?" I can't keep the tremble of fear out of my voice.

"No," he reaches for my face, holding my cheek in his palm, looking me in the eyes as he tilts my face up to his. "I'm not leaving you."

I appreciate that small act of chivalry. The fact that he was nice enough to treat me this kindly after he rescued me. I know he's the man who protected me last night. Maybe it's the tiredness, but I suddenly don't trust that he's not ditching me.

Why would he stay?

And what happens to me if he goes?

"Please don't leave me," I feel my breath catch around the words. "I don't know where I am or who is coming. I'm—"

"Love," he leans over then, his lips brushing across my temple. The kiss is light and really comforting. "Remember last night when I promised you that I wouldn't let you go to Vincent's bed? And then I promised to take you with me?"

"Yeah."

"I promise to come back. Okay?"

"Okay." My eyes mist with tears. He presses the room key into my hand.

"It's going to take me a bit since I'll have to walk back. Try not to worry."

"Okay." I rub a tired hand down my face, trying to hide the fact I'm about to cry. I know I'm being stupid, but I squeeze his hand even tighter like I'm not going to let go. I nip at my lip leaning forward.

His eyes in the morning light are gray and absolutely gorgeous. Like mesmerizing. "Kate. I'm coming back for you."

"Promise?" I know he already promised. "I'm sorry. I'm just tired and I don't know where I am. I don't have any money or a phone or even clothes. I…" I stop when his thumb strokes over my cheek.

"I promise." And then he kisses me on the lips. It's the lightest brush of his mouth but the whole world freezes. He leans back but I'm still leaning way out, my body craning toward his, waiting for another taste.

I finally pull myself together, settling myself back in my seat. "Thank you," I whisper.

"Now get inside. I'll leave as soon as I know you've deadbolted the door."

With a nod I finally let go of his hand, pushing open the car door.

No one is out, it's still ridiculously early, which is a good thing because I look awful. I slide the key into the lock and the door swings open.

Stepping into the dark interior, I close the door and bolt it behind me. Peeking through the curtain, I watch the Fit back out of the parking spot and drive away.

What will I do if he doesn't come back?

Swallowing down a lump, I head into the bathroom as I try to decide. I look in the mirror to see dark circles under my eyes. My hair isn't as bad as I thought. I take several deep breaths as I think.

If Luke doesn't come back, I'll go to the front desk and call Mark. He's had the same number for the last fifteen years. And he's the only man I've ever been able to rely on. He'd come get me, I'm sure of it.

I could hole up at a Vegas hotel while I start my internship. Vincent and Vigo picked me up at my shithole apartment so I don't think I can go back there. Which totally sucks. It was so hard to find a place that cheap, but it's a problem for later.

These thoughts help calm me as I start the shower. The towels are the size of postage stamps and tiles are missing from the wall, but the tub is clean.

I stick my hand under the spray, the water is even hot.

I strip off my bathrobe and dress, plucking the contacts from my eyes. I can't see distance without them, but I just can't wear them anymore. At home I have glasses…

With a sigh, I step into the spray. The shampoo and conditioner are of terrible quality but they get the job done, and I get out a half hour later realizing that I feel way more human.

I wrap one of the towels around me, but it barely covers my ass, and I try to tuck one end into my cleavage.

If there is one asset I've always had, it's boobs. The towel barely tucks around them.

I finger-comb my hair, knowing it's not going to do me any favors later. I'm going to look even more like a sewer rat.

In an attempt to help, I go into the bathroom and break out the blow dryer.

My hair is mostly straight, but I've got a wave here or there that needs to be ironed out. Or diffused to be curly.

A noise makes me turn off the dryer.

Was that a knock?

Creeping across the room, I peek through the closed blind. Luke stands at the door, his face set in hard lines.

Relief makes me limp as I unlock the deadbolt and open the door, a wide smile on my face. I'm so happy to see him. I had a plan, but I'm so glad he's back.

He blinks for one second, and then his eyes skate down my body, the tiny towel all that's covering me.

I feel the flood of heat in my cheeks as he steps inside, two bags in his injured hand, three in the other. He kicks it closed and sets down the bags, locking the door again.

Then he turns to me, hooking my waist and pulling me up against his chest. "That's quite the greeting, love."

I grab his biceps, turning my face to the side. "Sorry. I didn't have anything else to wear."

But my embarrassment is rapidly evaporating, that ache starting to pulse between my legs again.

His nose brushes my neck, just below my ear. "No apology needed."

"You came back."

"I told you I would."

I feel myself melting into him. I should put on clothes. "Did you um…bring me anything to wear?"

"This towel is working just fine," he murmurs into my skin, the deep vibration of his voice humming through me.

"I…we…" I swallow down a lump. We're both exhausted, we're being chased. This is hardly the time for a hook up, but even thinking the words *hook up* has my nipples tightening and I know he feels it the way he smiles against my skin.

"I brought you clothes. And food too." His hand at the small of my back runs down over my ass, brushing the bare skin at the back of my thigh. I gasp in a small breath, the touch of his fingers causing a shower of tingles to pulse through me.

He fans the fingers out, skating them back up under the towel, tracing my inner thigh.

It's the most erotic thing a man has ever done to me, though to be fair, my experience is rather limited.

But how can a man's fingertips on my skin be this amazing? My breath is coming out in these tiny gasps, my pulse rushing in my ears.

He stops just before he's touching my sex, his fingers pressing into the softness of my skin.

I close my eyes, tipping my head further back like I'm giving him all the access he needs. Because I know that sex with Luke would just be amazing…

He places a tickling kiss just under my ear. "Since you were out on a date, I'm assuming there's no boyfriend?"

"No. I don't really…I mean I'm so busy…I…" I can't even form a sentence as his tongue joins his lips, licking and kissing down the skin of my neck. "You?"

"We both know I'm not boyfriend material."

No. He isn't. My hips contract, pressing deeper into his pelvis as I shamelessly try to get him to bring his fingers just a little higher.

I can feel his cock pressing into me. Is it my imagination or is it large? Like really big?

Boyfriend material? Who cares?

Not me.

Is this the way I planned to lose my virginity? Nope. But I'm not sure I care. I'm tired of being the oldest virgin on Earth, and besides, this isn't real life. This is some crazy alternate reality.

I ignore the voice that tells me I'm making the exact mistake I promised myself I wouldn't ever commit.

His lips reach my collarbone, his tongue gliding along my skin. "You taste delicious, Kate."

God, I want to taste him too. Like lick a path down his body until I'm swallowing him whole. I give myself a little shake.

I've never been like this. I stiffen away at the thought, and he lets me go. "Help yourself to the clothes and the food. I'm just going to take a quick shower."

And then he's gone, sauntering into the bathroom. Did I just dream that heated encounter?

The slick heat coating my thighs says no.

Shaking it off, I open up the bag that looks like clothes and find packs of T-shirts, underwear, and socks for him. How long does he think we're going to be gone? In the second is stuff for me. A tiny little tank and shorts for sleeping, plus jeans, shirts, etc. There is even a pair of ballet flats and sneakers, both which look like they'll fit.

Taking the pajamas off the hanger, I slip them on and open a third bag with toothbrushes, a hairbrush, and elastics.

Grabbing up the brush, I run it through my hair.

The last bag has food and I grab a power bar, ripping it open and taking a big bite. Dinner was hours ago, and I've been up all night.

Taking several more bites, I feel my brain start to work again as I crack open a water bottle and take a swig.

That's when I turn and look at the bed.

The one bed.

How did I miss that detail in the last hour I'd been in the room?

The shower goes off and this time it's Luke who comes out in a low-slung towel and nothing else.

Dear merciful lord in heaven, the man is everything I've ever imagined. Like if I created a sex fantasy, he would be it.

He's now sporting a five o'clock shadow on his strong, sexy jaw, His wet hair is pushed back from his face, curling slightly around his ears and softening the hard planes of his face the slightest bit.

His shoulders are ridiculously broad and the tattoos... I must have been in shock last night to have missed the sleeve of them on his shoulder and arm. My gaze travels down his torso. He's cut muscle all the way down to where they disappear under the towel.

I would love to see what's underneath. "Umm," I start, swallowing a lump.

His eyes scan down me. "That looks adorable on you."

I wince at the word adorable. I've always been pretty. Cute. Adorable. I've got nice legs and boobs.

And my features are pretty classic. They just come off more "girl next door" and less Hollywood starlet. Just this once, I'd like to be the kind of girl who oozes sex appeal. "Thanks but…" I point to the bed. "I just realized we've only got the one. Bed. One bed."

He looks over at the bed and shrugs. "All right."

"Well, it's just…" Crap. I'm blushing again.

"It's fine, love. I make an excellent pillow." And then he crosses to the Walmart bag and bends down. I stare at him, my mouth agape, as he rummages through the bag one-handed.

He pulls out the package of underwear, trying to open it with the hand on his one good arm. He's been using his injured arm all night. It must be killing him.

"Shit," I mutter. Here he is, taking care of me, buying me clothes and I'm not helping him at all. "Give me that."

I tear open the package and pull out the underwear, unrolling it, and pulling off a sticky tag.

Then I hold them out to him.

He quirks a brow. "You wouldn't mind helping a guy into them, would you?"

My mouth drops open. I can see how it would be difficult with a hurt shoulder, but that would mean I'd have to bend down with my face right by his… "Sure. Yeah. No problem."

I bend, holding the underwear open. He steps one leg in and then the other. He's so close and the tent that's forming in the towel is not helping me keep my focus. "Pull them up for me?"

"Yeah." I start automatically, my hands sliding along the rough hair of his legs. God, his muscles feel so good. I end up slowing down just to savor the feel of him.

I get them up around his thighs, but my hands are pushing at the edges of the towel, and then, in slow motion, the towel just falls to the floor.

And there it is.

I'm staring at his bulging cock a few inches from my face.

I fall back, my butt landing on the floor, as a gasp falls from my lips.

"I know," he winks down at me. "Impressive, right?"

"Ass," I mutter, but honestly, it's an amazing cock. Do they all look that good? Thick, long, a few bulging veins that just make it even more…

He reaches his good hand down for mine and I place my fingers in his, letting him pull me up.

"I'll stay on my side of the bed," his grin widens. "If you can stay on yours." And then he lets go of my hand, pulling first one side of the underwear up and then the other up over his hips, trapping the monster in the black fabric. I have the most ridiculous urge to take that underwear back off.

Except it's a terrible idea, and as I look over at the bed, a jaw-splitting yawn falls from my lips.

"It's a deal," I mutter, and start toward the bed and stop again. "Which side?"

"I'll take the one by the door, sweetheart. Always." His hand comes to the small of my back, "And if there's trouble, you roll off the edge and hide. Understand?"

Those words make my chest tight. Is he sleeping next to the door to protect me? My ovaries practically explode as I turn back to look at him over my shoulder. My lips part as I try to think of how to say how much I appreciate all he's done. Thank you is getting old. "Luke, I..."

His hand slides around my waist to my belly. He doesn't pull me close, but his fingers spread out, covering my entire stomach. "Let's get some sleep, sweetheart."

I nod and then take a step forward, slipping from his grasp as I make my way around the bed and pull back the covers.

Sliding into the sheets, I sigh as my head hits the pillow. Then I lift my head up again. "I had one of the power bars and some water." I sit up again. "You want one too?"

He's still standing where I left him, in nothing but the black boxer briefs I just slid up his legs. His legs are in this wide stance, his shoulders broad. My mouth goes dry and I nearly regret not just closing my eyes.

How am I going to sleep next to him?

"A power bar would be great."

Nodding, I get up from the bed and pad across the floor, back by him, to the bag of supplies. I open the water and hand it to him. Then I grab a bar and part the wrapper.

He takes a long swig of water, sets the open bottle on the nightstand, and grabs the power bar. "Thanks. Arm hurts like a bitch and my fingers are really weak this morning. Carrying the bags might have been a bad idea."

"You likely have a bruised or pulled tendon," I murmur. "I can check it if you want."

"Later." He gives me a long stare that somehow feels more intimate than sliding underwear up his legs or even having his junk in my face. "Get in bed, love."

"You sure you're good?"

"I'm good."

I nod and slip back into my spot on the bed. I close my eyes and despite thinking I might never fall asleep, my eyes blink shut, desperate to close.

Luke still stands in the center of the room, his eyes on me as I drift away.

CHAPTER FIVE

Luke

Jesus fucking Christ, she's gorgeous. Kate sighs as she instantly falls asleep, that curtain of dark hair fanning out over her pillow.

She's not my usual style. But then again, my usual style of woman is fast, easy, and gone in the morning.

I know Kate is not that girl.

Would she let me fuck her? Yeah, she would. I had my fingers on her thigh and her skin was already slick with her arousal dripping down her leg. It was so hot, it took every ounce of my self-control to keep my fingers from sliding higher. I could have just plunged them inside her. I know she would have been hot, wet, and so fucking ready for me.

I wanted to and I know she wants it too. The problem is my reaction to her. It's the way she moves, how delicate her hands are, how pretty she is down to every tiny detail.

There is something so fragile and delicate in her beauty that it brings out every male instinct I have. I felt it's pull from the very first second.

I know burying myself deep in a woman like that is bound to cause problems. I've always been the least important cog in the Kincaid wheel. Now, with Roman hurt, maybe worse, they deserve my undivided allegiance and efforts. I should come up with a plan.

Then again, I'm more of an act-first-think-later kind of guy.

I pull back the covers and get into the bed, Kate lets out another sigh. Even the sounds of her little sighs are soft and sweet.

I lay on my right side facing her and blocking her from the door as I just watch her.

Her lips are a full and pillowy, the pale pink color perfect against her smooth, fresh skin.

She's got this tiny little nose that's perfectly straight and high arched brows. Her long dark lashes fan out on her cheeks.

The slant of her eyes is seductive, and their color is this rich brown that looks both warm and so fucking vulnerable.

And then there is the hair. Thick and long, it's so glossy that it looks like silk. I want it twisted up in my hands. I can just picture it wrapped around my fist while I plow into her. She's slender and I can picture how she'd look on top of me, my thick cock driving deep inside her while she cries out. My cock is so stiff, it starts leaking.

I know what she did for me is fucking with my head. We were in that room and her butterfly fingers flitted all over my skin, long and tapered, feeling so nice as she tended my wounds.

My dad split when I was young, but my mom is a strong woman, keeping both me and Roman in line after Roman's dad died. Took care of Roman's sister too. Though I know that one was a labor of love. Arabella and my mom still talk every day.

Christ, I hope Roman is all right. I can still hear the sound of his skull cracking on the pavement when he went down. I close my eyes, blocking out the view of Kate. I can't afford the distraction now.

Maybe I should fuck her. Get it out of my system. When I've blown a nut, I might be able to think again. Figure out how to help Roman.

My only comfort is that both Vigo and Vincent got into the car with me. Hopefully he came to and got out of there before Vigo could go back.

I shouldn't have dragged him out so late at night. It was my idea to go scope out of that house. But I'd fucked up the permits and I was trying to figure out how to fix my mistake.

Always so impulsive.

We're building a tunnel under the Las Vegas casinos. Casinos get to connect to our project by our grace and everyone knows, if we don't allow them access, their traffic is going to get cut.

The Italians took our lack of support personally, and it was personal.

When I said Roman's dad died, I meant he was murdered. And it was the Italians who did it. So yeah, there is no fucking way we're giving them anything except a trip to hell.

Kate is an innocent victim in all of this. And despite having the poor judgment to go on a date with Vincent, I do mean innocent.

I'm not an over-thinker. I don't get bogged down in shit. So I don't ask myself why, I just know that it's my job to see her through this. As long as it isn't at the expense of my family. I owe them everything.

I close my eyes. I just need a bit of sleep. An hour. Two. I got a map at Walmart and a burner phone too. I tried to get the number of Kincaid Enterprises but you need a credit card to pay for 411 and I don't want to leave a digital trail. I'm going to have track down a phone book...

And wheels.

One step at a time. That's how this shit gets done.

I fall asleep, too tired to think anymore.

I have no idea how long I'm out but when I wake...

I'm on my back, Kate is pressed into my side. Her leg and her arm are tossed over me, her hips grinding into the side of mine.

And her hand... Fuck me, it's stroking my raging cock.

"Love," I slur, half asleep. "That's some wake up."

"Mmm," she murmurs into my shoulder as she grips my hard-on through my briefs. "So good."

I look over at her, her eyes still closed, her lips softly parted and my eyes narrow. Is she still asleep?

Is she sleep-sexing me? This is way better than sleepwalking and I give a giddy grin, now wide awake. She's pinned my good hand to my side but I'm able to twist my wrist around just enough to slide a finger between her legs, pressing on her clit through her little sleep shorts.

She lets out a keening cry as she grinds into my finger. Can women cum in their sleep? Not sure why, but I kind of assumed they couldn't. Is today the day I get to find out?

I press a little harder, her head falling back as her body arches into my hand.

"I want you so bad," she mumbles, half garbled as she pants these little breaths. It's so fucking hot.

"Who do you want, baby? Say my name."

"Luke," she gasps. Oh, fuck yeah. She's sex-dreaming about me? Bring. It. On. And my experiment is forgotten as I back up enough to get my good arm under her and flip her onto my chest.

She lands hard enough that I wince in pain. Still totally worth it as her legs naturally fall on either side of my hips.

And then her eyes fly open. "Luke?"

"Yeah, love, it's me." And then I press up, pushing my cock right into her seam.

Her eyes roll back even as she sits up. "I don't… what…"

But her hands are on my chest, her fingertips digging into my skin.

"You had my cock in your hand. If you didn't mean it like that, now is your ditch out," I grind out between clenched teeth, pushing up into the heat of her pussy again.

Her pajama bottoms are still on, but I can feel how wet she is through the fabric.

Her skin is so pale, I watch the red creep up her exposed chest and infuse her cheeks. Is my girl embarrassed? She shouldn't be.

I reach up my good arm and fill my palm with her one of her ripe tits, the nipple instantly peaking through the fabric. "Want to take that tank off?" I ask, flicking her nipple with the nail of my thumb.

She arches again, embarrassment forgotten, as her head falls back, that long hair streaming down her back. "Luke."

"Yeah, baby, I'm right here. Take off the tank."

She does, both her hands grabbing the hem and yanking it over head.

Her nipples are the same pale pink as her lips, so fucking pretty, they make me ache.

Is her pussy the same color? The thought has me leaking cum as I take her now-bare tit in my hand again. I wish I could grab the other. Sleep has made the injured arm even weaker and if I want the damn thing to get better, I've got to rest it.

But I use my one good hand to feel one and then the other as she grinds against me.

I haven't mock-fucked like this in years and I got to be honest, it's fucking hot. I could do this all morning or afternoon, whatever time it is, but I can't get too lost in the moment. Which is why I grunt. "Pull my underwear down."

She lifts up, yanking them down my hips to my thighs. They don't need to go any farther, that's good enough.

I already know she's not wearing underwear under the shorts. Does she always sleep like that or was she just too tired? Mysteries to ponder later. "Push your shorts to the side and sink down on me sweetheart. Take my cock."

Yeah. I'm fucking bossy. I get it.

Most women submit in the bedroom to my commands.

But Kate…

She lets out this high-pitched whimper at my rough tone, her nipples getting even tighter.

She isn't just submitting. She likes it. And she does what I've told her to do without a second thought, pushing those little shorts to the side and lifting up so that she can sink down on my hard on.

Fuck. Me. She feels so fucking good. Tight, hot, wet. So tight. She wraps me up in her sheath, taking me in a quick thrust that has my eyes closing.

Which is why I almost miss the way she stiffens. Almost. My eyes open to see her features twist in pain.

No fucking way.

"Kate." It's a command. A demand.

She knows it. "I'm sorry." Her lips are trembling, her body folding in on itself.

Is she apologizing to me? She starts to lift off and I look down at my cock slick with her blood. She was a virgin.

My hand comes to her hip, stopping her. Does she think she's getting off now? "Don't apologize, love." I pull her down on my chest, my lips coming to the crown of her head. That is not how a man should take a woman's virginity. "If I'd known, I would have gone a lot slower."

She shakes her head against my chest. "I liked it."

Okay, I'm trying to be a gentleman here but that just gets my motor going all over again. Slowly, I flex my hips to pull out of her and then push back in. She's still stiff, but I keep it light, gentle, until I feel her hips flex too. That's it, baby. Come to Luke.

I push in a little deeper and she gasps, but not in pain. This one she likes. With a satisfied growl I hold her hip and push inside her again.

She tightens around me, letting out a needy little moan. And then she pushes back up, her body arching in the sexiest fucking way. She moans like I feel that good too.

Her hands settle back on my chest, they look so small and perfect, her pale skin practically glowing against my dark skin and ever-darker chest hair.

And then she lifts herself up, moaning as she slides back down, her head undulating in a slow circle that swings her hair. "I don't think," she lets out this little hitching breath. "I don't think I'm going to last very long."

Have I got her all hot and bothered? Fuck yeah, I do. I didn't get to see that sweet little pussy, but if she wants to cum, I'm going to feel it with more than my cock.

I slide my good hand, palm up between us, so my fingers are

spreading her lips even wider and when she comes down, the heel of my hand digs right into her clit.

Like a fucking bomb, she goes off, her whole pussy clenching me so tightly, my vision blurs.

She lets out a keening cry that I swear, half the motel must hear.

A few more pumps, and I'm ready to blow too.

"Love, you've got to get off," I press out between gritted teeth.

But she's still coming down from her high, her foggy, unfocused eyes not registering what I've said.

I push up with my hand, my shoulder twinging like a bitch, but I just get her off my cock just as I start spraying cum first on her thighs and then over my own stomach.

She gasps, her wide eyes meeting mine. "Shit. Luke."

It's my turn to barely register.

It's another I haven't in forever… I haven't cum without anything or anyone touching me since I was maybe thirteen and I'd wake up covered in jiz.

What is Kate doing to me?

I look down and it's an absolute mess. Blood. Cum. Holy crap, it's fantastic. She looks too but her eyes are filled with horror. "Oh my God."

"Yeah. We did that right."

"Right?" she whispers. "First, I was just touching you in your sleep and then I nearly missed on the whole *get off my cock so I don't cum inside you*," she points at the mess on my stomach. "And I forgot to tell you that I was a…"

I reach for her waist, pulling her down on top of me so that those gorgeous tits are pressed to my chest, and so that my cum is on her stomach too. I think I've ruined those little shorts beyond repair.

Might carry them around in my pocket.

"Do I seem upset?"

She gives me a small smile. "No. But still. I think I might suck at this."

"I think you're very good at it. But we can work sucking in next time."

Her face flushes again. I love how easy she is to make blush. I've never been into blushing women before, but there is something about Kate that just makes me want to fluster her as much as possible.

"We should not do that again," she whispers.

My jaw clenches as I roll her to the side. There have been plenty of women who have tried to catch me. But let's be honest, they like the money. Maybe they even like the swagger. Or the looks.

And it's usually me that's saying, *This was fun, maybe I'll catch you around sometime.* I don't like receiving the line.

But it's probably for the best. I've got my family to help. I can't get distracted now.

Mason and Roman are the brains.

Leo is the fire.

My uncle Jake is the man who keeps us all safe.

And me.

I'm a good time. They cut me in because I'm family. Because I was in their circle, but I don't bring much to the table.

I swing my feet to the floor as I sit up, my back to Kate as I push up from the bed.

"Luke?"

I turn back to find her propped on her elbows, her tits looking amazing as that hair streams out behind her.

She's nipping at her lip, her eyes worried. "Are you upset with me?"

Not her. I was upset with myself. I bend down, balancing on the good arm as I kiss her lips. "No. Not upset."

"Okay. But you got up really quick and—"

I pull back just far enough to talk. "We're in a bit of a rush today."

"Oh. Right."

I kiss her again because she tastes delicious. And because even though I was busy being all offended, she's the one who just gave me her virginity. I pack that one away to think about later, but right now, she deserves a bit of tenderness.

I kiss her a third time and her mouth melts into mine, her fingers sliding through my hair. When I finally pull back, her eyes looked glazed again.

She can tell me all she wants we shouldn't have sex again, the truth is in her unfocused eyes.

One side of my mouth quirks up. "Ready for a shower?"

She flushes again. "That sounds great," she twists her hands together, scooting toward the edge of the bed. "You're cool with a one-time thing?"

I stand up. I've got myself a good girl. One who seems to have gone crazy for my dick. And is trying to convince me that we should keep it casual. If it weren't for the whole "being chased by murdering twins" part, I'd be in heaven. Then again, I can handle Vincent and Vigo. And Gorilla too. "I'm cool, baby girl."

"And my touching you in your sleep..." She flushes again.

"You touch my dick anytime you want. No apologies required."

And then I pull her toward the shower. "I'm gonna clean us both up, and while you're getting yourself together, I'm gonna see if I can find us some coffee and wheels."

"Are we lifting another car?"

I glare at her. I live in the gray, she's not joining me. On that, I am crystal clear. "We are not doing anything. I'm going to buy a car." Hopefully.

"With a thousand bucks?"

"Eight hundred." Walmart burned through a couple bills.

I step into the bathroom and turn on the shower.

It's time to get moving. I've got a girl I need to keep safe and a family to save.

CHAPTER SIX

Luke

When I come back out of the shower, Kate's dressed with her wet hair hanging down her back. She's sitting on the bed with her knees drawn up to her chest. Her eyes are wide as they follow me. I know she's worried.

I just can't quite pinpoint why.

That I'll leave. That I'll fuck her again. That I won't.

It's probably because she's leagues smarter than me. But I do have some sense, sense enough, with the towel still slung around my hips, to stop by the bed and lean down, giving her a long slow kiss.

It's to soothe her, but I like it too.

Her lips are so fucking soft, and she tastes delicious. I don't know how she managed it, but she's got this fresh citrus flavor. Dipping into her mouth a few times, I finally pull back.

"I want to come with you." She's biting her lip again. It's vulnerable and sexy and I brush my thumb over her sweet lips.

"I'll be back soon. Dry your hair. Relax."

She pushes off the bed and I catch a whiff of sex still hanging in the air. Her. Me. I'm growling as I pull her close. So much for the *fuck her one time and get her out of my system* theory. Then again, I've never taken a girl's virginity before. It was fucking hot, even hotter knowing that she's mine. Only mine.

Her hands splay out on the cords of my neck. "Every time you go, I worry you won't come back." The words are whispered, the fear in her eyes real.

"What did I tell you, love? I promised. I'm coming back."

She gives a tentative nod, even as she pushes up on her toes, and kisses me again. Pressed against me, I feel her tremble and it kind of wrecks me.

Gathering her in my arm, I press her close. "Hey. You think I'm gonna let a fuck that good be a one-time thing?"

She laughs a little shaking her head. "It is a one-time thing. Remember?" Her gaze slides to the side. "I made a plan when you left yesterday. What I would do if you didn't come back..."

Of course she did. She's a smart woman.

But I still hear myself saying, "It's me and you, love. We're riding this wave."

She smiles and shakes her head. "Okay. You're coming back. Just..." She blows a breath. "Be careful, all right?"

Worried about me? "I will, baby. Don't worry."

"Want me to check that shoulder?"

"Later. I want to get out of here and I have no idea how long our errands will take."

She nods.

I pull her close again. "In the unlikely event that any of our friends from last night show up, go out the bathroom window and walk to Walmart. Meet me in sporting goods."

"Sporting goods? Why there?"

"They've got good shit." And then I wink. "Any thoughts on who might have a phone book around? Walmart did not."

"Hmmm. A local place probably. Something old-school."

"That's good thinking." I run a hand through my damp hair. "Last question. How do you take your coffee?"

"Black."

I didn't see that one coming.

"Med student. We stay up all night, and we don't spike our blood sugar with milk."

"Fair enough."

And then I lean into the Walmart bag and pull out a fresh T-shirt and briefs. My jeans go back on and my shit-kicking boots. Kate watches me, softly nipping at her bottom lip. When I'm about to tie up my boots, she bends down and does it for me.

I can't help it, my hand threads into her hair, stroking down the long length. Finally, I stand, crossing my arms. "How do I look?"

"Fantastic," she mumbles as she stands. I catch the flush before she turns away. One corner of my mouth tilts up. I look down at my boots, kicking one with the other.

They were expensive once upon a time, but I've worn the hell out of them.

Leo likes designer casual wear. Roman and Mason are all high-end suits. Jake is old school and wears whatever he wants.

But me… I like ripped jeans, old boots. I like a little wear and tear with my fashion, and so I smooth a hand down my Walmart T-shirt like I'm the boss.

It does a decent stretch across the shoulders. Not too shabby.

"All right." I roll my shoulders, getting ready to face the world and get my shit done. "I'll be right back, love."

"Bye," she turns to the bathroom, but I don't miss the way she looks back over her shoulder at me. I give her perfect ass one last glance before I'm out the door.

Making my way down the street, I look like any guy in worn jeans and scuffed boots, except I'm new and I know I'm good-looking, so I get a few looks. I'm just about thinking I've got to go on a side street when I see a couple standing outside a gas station, in front of an old beat-up pick-up truck with the hood open.

"I told you not to buy this thing," the woman huffs. "Piece of junk."

"It was free, Alice."

"Free," she says back. "It breaks down every time we drive it. It's been anything but free."

The guy scratches his head. "I never was good at repairs."

Luck be a lady, I grin. And I'm a girl magnet. "Hey there," I call out. "Truck trouble?"

The guy looks relieved. "Know anything about this kind of engine?"

"Love these oldies with their carburetors and their leaky oil," I wink as the woman, Alice I think her name was, rolls her eyes.

"What's the trouble?"

"Won't start. Again."

"Let me have a look." I climb up and move a few wires, check the oil. Spark plugs are gone which is likely the issue. They're a cheap fix too, but I'm not telling this guy that. I whistle through my teeth. "It's not good."

"I knew it!" Alice cries, her hands flying up in the air.

"How bad?" the guy asks. "How much?"

"Couldn't say. With time and money, she'll run again…"

"No," Alice hisses. "No more money."

"Didn't catch your name," I say to the man. "Mine's Jake." I use my uncle's name just in case.

"Jake?" He cocks a brow. "Pleased to meet you. Clyde."

"Clyde. A pleasure." I stick out my hand and we shake. Then I look back into the truck's engine bay. "A truck like this can be a real gem." I'm not lying. "But she's going to require a lot of tender loving care."

Clyde makes a face. "I've only got room for one high maintenance lady in my life."

"I heard that," Alice says, hands on hips. Then she stomps into the station.

"You ah…" Clyde scratches his head. "You wouldn't be interested in a gem like this?"

Now, here is the part where I really need to work it hard. I've only got so much cash and Kate and I are going to need to eat.

Maybe buy a few more pajama sets.

"I'd love a truck like this but the money..." I click my tongue. "I just don't have it, Clyde."

He looks me up and down and nods. "How much you think you could spare?"

I shake my head. We're starting this negotiation from zero.

Clyde takes the bait. "Look. Just give me enough to take Alice out to dinner. Nothing fancy. I tried to give the damn thing to my brother, and he wouldn't take it."

"I appreciate what you're saying Clyde, but..." I shake my head a few times. "I'm a little hard up." I'm being a dick. But I don't know how long Kate and I are going to have to live off what I've got.

He leans in close. "It pisses her off sitting in the yard. It makes her even madder when we drive it anywhere." He goes around to the glove box and takes out a title. "I'll let you have it if I can tell Alice you paid me."

I give him a wicked grin. "You got it, Clyde. It's a deal." And then we shake again.

His name is on the title, and I make a note to send Clyde a big thank you later. Pocketing the title—who leaves that shit in the car, Clyde—I head down the street to a tiny automotive store and grab spark plugs and oil.

Then, the coffee shop, for two black coffees.

I'm giddy as I head back to the truck. This is my jam. Hood is still open, and I pull out the plugs, blowing on them, and top off the oil.

I've decided to name her Alice and I'm thinking that this might be the luckiest day ever.

I got laid, I've got a pretty lady looking at me with big brown eyes begging me to stay, and now I've got a truck. And coffee.

That's when I catch a flash of red out of the corner of my eye.

I turn and catch a fucking GT3 heading toward Walmart.

Fuck. No one around here owns a car like that. It came from Vegas. No doubt.

Turning over the engine, Alice fires up, a deep rumble that should be satisfying but isn't, and I put her into gear, backing out of the spot.

I'm really hoping that Clyde has already left and the real Alice is not witnessing me pulling the free truck out.

Because if she is, Clyde is not getting any for a while. But I can't worry about my man now.

Instead, I follow the GT3. Maybe I should just go back to the motel, but I need to see how bad this is. If one of the Italians found me here, they are watching closely and they are on the hunt.

I'm the lynchpin to their plan. I know it. They want to use me to gain access to the tunnel.

I could turn myself back over to them. That would honestly be best for Kate. Vincent would likely forget all about her. But my family…

Getting caught is the worst that can happen. These assholes would use me to blackmail Kincaid Enterprises. I know that was the plan. The very least I can do is stay out of the way, keep Gorilla distracted.

It would be even better if I could find a way to push those permits through. But I have to trust that Mason is on top of that shit.

I could disappear on my own. They'd follow me, not her. But it's way easier to stay under the radar with a girl on my arm. We're on a couple's getaway. I'm using her and I know it, but she's the one who begged me not to leave her.

I should cut her loose, I know it deep in my gut. But part of me isn't ready to let her go, and like I said, I'm giving her what she asked for. Why should I feel guilty for that?

I don't even make it all the way to Walmart when I see the squad car lights flashing blue.

Popping open a compartment on the dash of the truck, I find a beat-up pair of aviator sunglasses and I put them on, ducking low in the seat.

The GT3 pulls up next to the cop car and out pops Gorilla. Asshole.

I don't know how he got out of the cord I tied him up in, or how he found me, maybe the Fit had a GPS tracker, but I know it's time to get the hell out of Dodge. Or whatever town we're in.

At the next light I make a right and then another and a third until I've reversed direction.

Pulling into the motel, I take a deep breath. I should tell Kate to go back to Vegas. Stay with a friend. Lay low...

That's what would be best for her...

I get out of the truck and start for the door, which cracks open before I can even knock. I stop. "You all right, love?"

She opens the door a little wider. "Just glad you're back." Her smile is easy. Relieved. My gut twists.

Pushing into the room, I can also see that she's collected up all our stuff, packed it back in the bags, and we're ready to roll.

God, I love a competent woman. "Where'd you get the truck?"

"I'll tell you on the way. Let's roll."

"Okay," she says grabbing up a couple of the bags. "Where are we going?"

"We'll decide that on the way too."

She cocks her head and looks at me. "Something happen?"

"On the way, love," I answer, grabbing the other bags. She gives me a single nod, her face pinching as I walk her quickly out to the truck.

I can barely appreciate how hot she looks in her tight jeans as she climbs up into the passenger's seat.

Closing her door, I make my way around the driver's side and fire up Alice. "We've got some choices," I say, tossing the old truck in gear. We're not getting anywhere fast, but then again, who's going to suspect the guy in the 1970s two-toned beige-and-cream Ford is a billionaire real estate mogul? "Keep going east or head back to Vegas."

"I've got three days until I have to be back for work," she tells me. "Which way do you think is safer?"

I frown. That's a tricky question because my answer is different from hers. "Away from Vegas. I say we keep moving east."

"East it is," she smiles. "Actually, one of my stepdads has a cabin in southern Colorado. We could crash there for a few nights."

"One of?"

"You don't want to know," she mutters.

"Sounds like a good story for on the way. Mind breaking out the map and telling me which direction we're headed?"

"Right. I'm navigator." She rummages through the bags. "But you're taking a left just up here. We're for sure headed back toward the interstate."

I don't take the left. Because that would take us right by Walmart.

When I miss it, she sits up and gives me the eye. "You really are bad with directions."

I wink. "I'll be better next time."

Pulling out the map, she starts checking our route and I take the next left.

Kate and I are headed to Colorado. Didn't see that one coming.

But even with my Gorilla sighting, I'm not sure I'm upset about this road trip. Fucked up as this is, it might be the most fun I've had in a long damn time.

But I'll unpack that one later.

We find the highway and I take the eastbound on-ramp, Alice bumping along. No AC in a car like this, so we roll down the windows, the desert heat making it a hot day and the wind making conversation difficult. It's all right, though. I'd rather wait until we're far away from whatever little town that was to tell Kate that Gorilla is on our tail.

I don't want my girl to worry.

Yet.

CHAPTER SEVEN

KATE

LUKE LOOKS good in this truck.

I mean, really good. What is it about a little retro, a little dinge that just suits him?

The sunglasses rest on his nose as he leans back in the seat, driving with one hand, the good one.

I'd offer to drive but he doesn't look uncomfortable at all. "How's your arm?" I yell over the wind blowing through the truck.

It's got to be pushing a hundred degrees out there so we can't close the windows. "Fine, love," he grins over at me, that one-sided sexy-as-hell, bad-boy grin that sends my stomach fluttering.

I know the arm can't be fine, but you'd never know it looking at him. How do guys do that? How does he do it?

My fingers itch to undo the lap belt and slide over the bench seat. I'd press against his arm, and he'd kiss me. I let out a sigh.

It's a dumb idea. I've seen my mom date a million bad boys. It always ends the same.

He gets bored, or meets someone better, and I'm left broken. He never would have even looked my way if we hadn't been forced together.

I'm sure the adventure of running is fueling whatever is between us.

Placing my hands in my lap, I squeeze them together, trying to keep my eyes to myself, but they keep drifting to him.

"Shorty, if you keep looking at me like that, I'm gonna pull this truck over and fuck you on the side of the road."

He has this way of making me blush and I do now. Because that sounds hot. "Luke." I can't even tell if I'm chastising or encouraging him.

His eyes scan down my body, and I can see him considering. "I'm going to keep driving, love. I want to put as much distance as possible between us and them."

"You think they'll follow?" He grimaces in a way that makes my stomach churn in the worst way. "What's wrong?"

"They did follow. I saw Gorilla in the Walmart parking lot."

"Shit!" I cry, gripping his arm. "How?"

"GPS on the Fit. I knew it was a possibility."

I stare at him. "That's why you parked it away from the motel last night."

He nods.

Like I need any more evidence that Luke is trouble. I always secretly knew I liked trouble. Hence my lack of dating experience.

I let out a long rush of air. "Well, this truck probably isn't equipped with GPS."

"Nope. And I bought it fair and square."

I pull my chin back in disbelief. "You're not serious."

"I am, you should have seen me work that one." He reaches over and settles a hand on my upper thigh, his fingers dipping between my legs.

I stiffen away and he feels it,he looks over. "Want to tell me more about yourself?"

"Nope," I shake my head. We should not be getting to know each other.

"Should I tell you more about me?"

"Definitely not."

I want to lose myself in this man. I close my eyes, trying to be strong. "We should keep our conversations about escape. The plan."

He snorts. "Too late for that."

"Listen," I don't know what I'm building to, but I know I need to pump the breaks. I'm breaking every rule I ever made for myself.

"Shit," I hear him rumble, his voice vibrating through me.

I open my eyes, wondering what's wrong when I see a minivan pulled over to the side in front of us. My eyebrows furrow. "It's so hot. Why would anyone stop on a day like this?"

"Not by choice." He lets out a long, frustrated breath. I look at him, trying to figure out what he's thinking.

He glances down at me. "We need to make time but…"

"You want to pull over."

"There are probably kids in there," he rumbles, putting on the blinker of the truck. I want to respond, but I can hardly catch my breath, and once again, I swear, my ovaries explode. Saves women in need. Protects kids.

Who cares if he steals a car or two…

We pull over and he opens the door. "You should come just in case they need medical help."

I slide out too, taking his hand as we approach the car.

The door immediately opens and frantic and sweaty man steps out. "Thank you for stopping," he stumbles, and I curse under my breath. How long have they been sitting in the sun?

The other door opens, and a woman gets out, looking even worse than her husband. She seems disoriented as she tries to focus on me. "Kids?" I ask.

"Two," the dad hoarsely answers.

"Get them out. I've got water." But I'm already going around him and pulling on the minivan's sliding door. Both parents' reaction time is slow and I don't want to wait.

Two red-faced kids meet my gaze and I'm pulling the buckles open in the first kid's car seat.

"Should I have taken them out of the car?" the man asks, his voice filled with fear.

"No." I quickly smile back at him. "The direct sun is worse than the shaded car." I look at Luke. "Get the other boy."

He immediately starts around the car as I crack open the water, giving the little boy, who must be about four, a big swig. Then I pull him from the car. Two fingers on his throat, I check his pulse to see if it's elevated.

His eyes dilate as the sun hits them, a good sign, and I position him onto my hip as I carry the water to his mother.

"How long have you been here?"

"An hour and a half," the dad answers. "A few cars went by…" I grimace, then give the boy another drink and then hand the bottle to the mother. I turn to the dad. "How many fingers am I holding up?"

"What?"

"She's a doctor," Luke rumbles. "Answer." He's got the other boy, who looks six or seven, on his hip. My eyes linger for a second because… I've never seen anything more gorgeous than this man holding a kid.

The dad looks at me. "Three."

"Good." I turn back to Luke. "Get more water. I'm going to check everyone, but this little guy doesn't have heatstroke. Dehydration, however, is a real concern."

He nods and goes get two more bottles. We'll have to buy more when we get to the next town.

"What happened?"

"It overheated, I think?" the dad answers.

"I can look," Luke tosses over his shoulder as he goes to get the water. "Or we can all load into the truck and I can drive to you to the next town, get a tow truck."

The dad pauses for a second. "Can you just take a quick look?"

With a nod, Luke hands out more water and then gives the kid to his mother before he pops the hood. He winces. "You're out of coolant. But with these kinds of cars, you can't just dump water in them, and we're short anyway. Let me give you a ride."

Somehow, we all squish into the cab of the truck.

I'm pressed to Luke's side, the kids in the laps of their parents. Reaching down, I pass out power bars. They've sweat enough that I'm worried about replacing their body salt.

"I heard your stomach rumble," Luke says close to my ear. "I want you to eat one too."

There is only one left. I break it in half and pop half into my mouth. Then, I hold the second half up an inch from his lips. "We share."

One brow quirks before he takes the bite, sucking my fingers into his mouth too. I feel myself blush to my roots, especially since we have an audience, as I quickly withdraw my fingers.

But I'm hot and flushed, and it has nothing to do with the desert heat.

A half hour later, we roll up into a small town just as the sun starts to set. "Garage first, then the motel?" Luke asks the dad, whose name, we learn, is Carl.

Carl nods. "I can't thank you enough, man. You saved our lives."

"No trouble," Luke winks.

"Will we keep going after we drop them?" I softly ask.

Luke grimaces, cocking his head like he's thinking. Carl raises his hand. "Let me get you two a room for the night. It's the least I can do."

Luke thinks for a second and then gives a quick nod. "That's kind of you, Carl. I hope you don't mind me taking you up on the offer."

"Don't mind at all. Glad to give something back after what you did for us."

I look down at the four-year-old, Benji, who currently has chocolate all over his hands and face from the power bar. I smile at him, and he grins back. It's adorable.

He reaches a hand out to me, likely smearing some chocolate on my face. I laugh as I wrinkle my nose. Looking back, I catch Luke looking at me and I glance down at my lap.

Carl hires a tow truck and then we make our way to the smallest six-room motel I've ever seen.

Hungry as I am, I'm more tired, having only slept for a few hours the night before.

There's at least a McDonalds and Luke gets a burger while I munch on a few fries.

It's quiet between us, both of us tired, but it's a nice quiet. Not awkward at all, which is funny because we've only known each other for a few days now.

I'd like to lean on his shoulder and close my eyes, but I was the one trying to insert distance, so I keep myself upright, even as my stomach turns from exhaustion. He touches my knee under the table, and I smile at him as I take a bite of another fry. I can't help myself. But his look is one of concern. "You gonna eat more than that?" he asks, looking skeptically at my fries.

"Worried about me?" I tease.

He leans forward, not smiling. "Yes."

"I promise, the french fries are enough. I'm just tired."

He gives a nod. "Big breakfast tomorrow then."

My head cocks. I'm not used to people being worried about how much I eat. Not even my mom does that. Never did. But we leave and go back to the motel. The décor is sparse and old, but the place is clean, I'll give it that.

I brush my teeth and pull out a clean pair of underwear and a T-shirt. It's the best I'm going to do tonight.

Luke's eyes are on me as I start to climb into the bed.

"Stop," he murmurs. I've got one knee on the bed. My hands come down too and I turn to look back at him.

"Why?"

"Because," his grin is wicked, "I'm gonna help you sleep."

My brows lift even as my girl parts clench. "Luke. I don't know…"

He crosses the room, and hooks both hands on the sides of my underwear, sliding them over my hips.

Part of me meant it this morning when I said we shouldn't sleep together again. Everything is crazy and I am careening toward heartbreak.

But he slides the underwear down my legs to my knees. My whole body clenches in anticipation, all the exhaustion gone, but instead of touching me more, he steps back.

"What are you doing?" I gasp, almost covering myself as I fight my embarrassment.

"You have the prettiest fucking pussy I've ever seen," he growls. "I'm going to admire it for another second and then I'm going to mess it up real good, make it so dirty."

I swear, I'm drenched in a second.

His hand comes to my back, sliding up my spine over my neck to the back of my head. And then he gently pushes me down so my face is on the mattress, my ass in the air.

Any other guy, I'd be freaking out, but with him… I just do it, no questions, nothing but anticipation pulsing through me.

His fingers slide up the back of one of my legs, across my ass, and down the other. Goose pimples break out all over my flesh.

He starts back up the inside of my thigh and I squirm.

"For a girl who said we shouldn't do this, you're awfully impatient."

"Shouldn't is different than don't want to," I speak, my voice half muffled by the sheets.

He chuckles, his fingertips just brushing over my pussy. It's so light, I barely feel the touch. That doesn't keep me from starting to drip. "I don't even understand why we shouldn't."

He wouldn't. He's not the one who is going to get his heart broken.

He takes my silence as a cue to continue, and he brushes his fingers over me again with a bit more pressure.

"Did you know that you're the exact same color here," he slides a finger down my seam, "as you are on your nipples and your lips?"

"I…" It feels so good that I don't even know how to respond. I can't find the words.

"Funny, never thought I cared about matchy-matchy, but damn, love, you make it look good."

My hands twist into the sheets as his middle finger hits my clit.

I want to tell him that his compliment, along with his fingers, have me aching. But I'm beyond words.

I do know that I've wanted a guy like Luke to tell me I'm special my whole life. I know it's crazy and it shouldn't matter, but even that compliment sets me on fire.

And when his tongue replaces his finger, I let out a moan that I can't hold back.

And that's when I get a light smack on my ass.

CHAPTER EIGHT

Luke

I LOVE it when a woman makes noise. And I want nothing more than to make Kate fucking scream.

"Keep your face in the sheets, love, the boys are sleeping next door."

She looks back at me. "You're worried about the kids?"

Maybe. But I don't tell her that. Instead, I tip forward and lick her from one end to the other.

She is fucking delicious.

Her face plants into the sheets as she moans again, and I smile. "Such a good girl."

I hear her draw in a gasp as she lifts up again. "Is that a compliment?"

I give her a light smack on the ass again. "You bet your ass it is. Face down."

She does, and I reward her by swirling my tongue right over her clit.

I feel her quiver, her ass grinding back. Greedy little girl.

I slow it down, knowing that the torture will make the sex better later and that she's probably waking the kids with her screams. Fuck it. They aren't my kids. And the sounds she makes can practically make me cum, they're so good.

I'm still smacking her ass though. That shit's just fun.

I've been wondering if this morning was an anomaly. Like if Kate was just really amped up by all the danger and the adrenaline.

But her response this time is just as... enthusiastic. I've barely touched her and she's dripping wet and ready to cum.

She fucks me like she's starving.

I lick back down to her clit, sucking it between my teeth. She screams into the bed sheets, an orgasm ripping through her.

I'd love nothing more than to rip off my pants and sink balls deep inside her. Slam into her from behind. But I don't think I'm done teasing her yet.

Sinking a finger in her sopping pussy, she moans into the bed again, I place my hand along her seam so that my thumb presses into her clit and then, because I love the taste of her, I lick up her ass.

She's breathing into the bed like she might combust, and her insides start to convulse around my finger.

"Love, you know how to make a man feel good about himself," I say before diving back in.

She cums again, panting with the effort to keep quiet. Not that she's doing a good job.

But hey, A for effort.

I rip off my shirt, pulling at the button of my jeans when there is a knock at the door. "Fuck," I rumble.

Kate collapses on the bed and I toss the covers over her before I walk over to the window, peering out the crack between a broken blind. It's fucking Carl.

Pulling open the door, I leave the chain. "Hey, man. Need something?"

"Just... uh... checking on you two. Candy sent me over. We can... uh... hear some things and she was... uh... worried about Kate."

"Kate's fine," I give him a wolfish smile that's meant to tell him to fuck off. He doesn't, shifting on his feet.

"She sounds like she might be in distress."

I let out a long sigh. "Carl. You've got two kids. I know you know that Kate is fine."

"I might have two kids," he mutters, "but I've never heard sounds like that."

My chest puffs at that one. Cause yeah. I'm that good.

"Carl," Kate calls from under the covers. "Get lost."

Carl's eyes go wide for a second. "Now that, I heard."

I close the door with a chuckle, turning the deadbolt again. "Sorry, baby. I think we're going to have to make this quick."

She tosses off the covers and then resumes the position. My teeth grind together because Kate and I understand each other perfectly. My jeans only make it to my knees when I'm plunging my cock into her from behind.

We both moan as I bottom out.

Kate takes her hand and puts it over her mouth, but I just grit my teeth harder and start pumping into her like it's an Olympic sport.

I can already feel her trembling around me. Which only makes me pump harder. Kate has this way, I'm realizing, of making me work like I have never worked before.

She feels so good, I'm spitting and growling, trying to keep the sounds in.

She grabs a pillow and stuffs it under her face and then starts to moan like a woman possessed.

I'm guessing every tendon in my neck is about to snap as I use my injured arm to grab her hips, too oblivious to the pain, as I pump into her one, two, three more times before my balls fucking erupt.

I have no idea what sound even comes out of me, as I cum so hard, I can't even see. When I've shot every drop into her, we both collapse onto the bed.

Kate's still in her shirt, my pants are around my knees. "Next time we're getting completely naked first," I mutter.

And that's when I hear it.

The counter of the bathroom next door is squeaking. And then I hear a moan.

Apparently, Carl is going for baby number three. Good for him.

But that does remind me. "And tomorrow we need to hit a Walmart for condoms. I'm assuming you're not on the pill?"

"Walmart?" she asks, her face still in the pillow. "You really love that store. And I am."

I did my job right, because my girl barely moves, her eyes closing. "Hey. Walmart is good value, and seriously? You're on the pill?"

"Well, I was, until today. They're currently sitting on my bathroom counter, but I think we're good."

"Any particular reason?" It's probably none of my business but I just want to know stuff about her. Not sure why.

"So that I have regular periods." She turns over underneath me and I lift up a little to let her before I settle back down on her chest. Is it too late to pull her shirt off? I just like looking at her.

Which is another red flag. I just came until my balls turned inside out. I shouldn't be this interested in her body. That should have been satiated, but I'm already semi-hard just thinking about her tits.

"My turn to ask a question..." She hooks one of her legs around my hips and over my ass. I push her shirt up, kissing her chest just above her breast, wanting to taste her skin. "What do you do for a living?"

"Construction. Sort of." I know why I don't tell her about Kincaid Enterprises. Maybe I like that she doesn't know I'm rich. Or maybe I'm afraid she'll figure out that I should be dropping her off with some relatives. Not bringing her with me.

My hurt shoulder throbs, but it was totally worth it, as I put the pillow back under her head and get up to go get the bottle of ibuprofen.

She stretches. "What kind of construction?"

"Currently, I'm building a tunnel," I pop out a few pills, put them in my mouth, swig them down with water.

Her brow scrunches as she sits up. "Like do you run the equipment?"

Does she think I'm a crane operator or something? I know I don't come off as that smart, but why couldn't she peg me for a manager at least?

"And how does that make the Vendettis your rivals?"

"Love, you're supposed to be so tired after multiple orgasms, that you pass out."

She gives me a soft smile before she flops back on the bed, her hands stretching over that curtain of hair. I just stare, drinking her in. I can't get enough. "I should clean up."

"Don't get up." I tear my gaze away, and head for the bathroom, getting the washcloth myself and wetting it down. Returning to the bed, I nudge her knees open, wiping her down.

I've never taken care of a woman like this but then again, she'd do far more for me and has. "What's your place look like?"

She shrugs. "I've lived in Vegas for like two days, so that place has nothing but my suitcase. Back in New York, it was different. I've got no money, but I try to make my apartment cute. You know…"

I bet it's as adorable as her. I'd like to see it.

I return to the bathroom to rinse out the cloth and by the time I come out, she is sound asleep with the lights on, her shirt still pulled up, her arms over her head.

"That's right, baby girl. I wore you out." I turn out the light, climb into my side of the bed and pull her close, snuggling her into my side. She burrows down in, her skin like silk against mine.

I've never wanted long term. I don't know how to do relationships.

I barely have memories of my dad, what I know is that he left, and never came back. Never even sent a card.

It's not that I don't like women. My mom is the best person in the world. She raised me, Roman, and Arabella and never complained. Not a word.

Mason, he started making money and he sent Roman to college. Me, though, I wasn't going to have Mason pay for that and not my mom either. She'd worked like a dog just to keep food on the table until Mason started helping her out.

Besides, I just would have failed out of school. I'm not good at much.

When Mason pulled me into the first casino he bought, I was grateful for the job. But now, thirteen years later, I'm wondering what I've really done.

Do I just draft off other people?

What do I really have to give? I'm not smart. I don't make shit happen and I fuck up a lot. I've got money and looks, but even I know, that's not what a woman really needs to make her happy.

I have no clue how to make a relationship work. I can't even make my life work.

Maybe it's because I didn't have a dad around to show me how to do it on my own? Or maybe I take after him.

But either way…

I close my eyes wondering what's gotten into me. I never think like this.

I should find Kate's exit strategy, but I 'm not sure I want to let her go. I'll figure it out after I get Mason's number.

My family's got to come first.

CHAPTER NINE

Kate

The next morning we're pretty quiet as we get up, shower, and dress. The sex last night was… life changing.

I guess that's the thing about bad boys. Damn, do they feel good.

I'm quiet because I'm trying to figure a few things out. Am I following right in my mom's footsteps? Dating a man who is trouble?

And if he's not that kind of guy, how interested is he in me? Am I just convenient?

But when I finish drying my hair and step out of the bathroom, I realize Luke has been quiet too.

And that starts the pit in my stomach.

"Everything good with you?" I ask when our eyes meet. He's sitting on the bed, waiting for me to finish. I wish I had a little makeup. Maybe a styling brush.

He gives me an easy smile. "Good."

"It's just…" I clear my throat. "We haven't really talked much this morning."

He shrugs. "Sorry. Not much of a deep thinker."

"Sure," I nod like I get that. As a person who overthinks most things, I don't get it at all.

Is he just saying that? "You're, ah, not regretting last night, are you?"

He stands, his brows arching up. "Regret your face down in a pillow, your ass in the air while you came over and over?"

I'm hot all over in a second.

"No. I don't regret it." And then he's hooking my waist and pulling me close. The tension unwinds as our bodies press together. "But I am deciding what we might do as a follow-up tonight."

I should say no. This is a dangerous path I'm going down… "I want to try the sucking thing we discussed." Could I have told him I want to blow him any more awkwardly?

But honestly, I really do want to taste him. "You want to suck my cock?"

My tongue darts out to wet my lips. "Yes." And then our eyes meet.

He looks at me like a lion. Like he wants to devour me. Good.

Because there is one thing I know and that is that Luke has stuck around when I needed him most. That's a big thing for me.

He didn't leave me stranded. He's not taking my stuff, not that I have any. Which probably means I'm just in for a run-of-the-mill heartbreak. That's all fine.

I can handle that.

"Kate," he groans in my ear. "Baby. You're making it hard to leave this room."

"Am I?" Good.

But he still tugs me outside and helps me into the truck. We start down the road, silence falling again.

It wears on my nerves. This is why I didn't want a repeat. I can feel myself getting more insecure.

We stop at a diner, making our way inside for some breakfast.

"We can just have power bars," I say as a hostess shows us to a table. "I don't need a whole breakfast."

"Personally, I'm starving. Last night, I really worked up an appetite." He wiggles his eyebrows.

"Yeah… but… money. I'm used to eating out of vending machines, you know? It's no big deal."

Luke scowls. "Kate. I know we're living on a budget, but money isn't really an issue. We can afford this place. Trust me."

I'm the girl who went out with Vincent for a free dinner. My apartment is a complete dive. "I know you have a real job. I just…"

He cocks his head to the side. "Real job?"

That's when our waitress shows up. "What can I get for you, sugar?" She isn't talking to me.

She's tall, blonde, and leggy with curves for days. Not fat, just round in all the right places. She looks like she could be on a movie poster. What she's doing here, I have no idea. I just know she's everything I am not.

Luke barely glances at her, his eyes flicking down the menu. "We'll take two coffees. I'm getting the Hungry Man. What about you, love?"

The blonde's eyes narrow as she looks at me, her uniform so tight, she's got a whole lot of cleavage on display.

"I'm not hungry," I whisper, bile rising in my throat. This is the kind of woman I lose him to, I know it. That run-of-the-mill heartbreak is right around the corner.

"What? Don't be ridiculous." He takes my menu. "An egg over easy and whole wheat toast, for the lady."

"All right," the waitress gives him a big smile, but it isn't reaching her eyes.

Luke is studying me with a look of concern. "You don't want bacon or something?"

"No bacon," I shake my head.

"How about avocado. You need some good fats for energy." Then he looks at the waitress. "Got any avocado?"

She bats her eyes, giving him a smile like they share a secret. "For you, sugar, anything."

I roll my eyes as Luke hands over both our menus, all while she bats her eyelashes. But he doesn't even notice. He's still staring at me with his brow furrowed as the waitress leaves. "What was that about?"

I shrug, not really wanting to tell him. Looking down at my lap, I fiddle with my napkin. "She was really attractive."

"Was she? I didn't notice."

My head lifts back up and then cocks to the side. "Well, good thing I pointed it out then." Irritation skitters up my spine, but I don't know who I'm mad at. Maybe myself.

He's staring at me like I've lost my mind. I probably have. "Kate."

I actually feel some silly tears welling in my eyes. "I'm just going to go the bathroom. Be right back."

I hop up from the table and race to the bathroom, trying to hide my face.

Locking the door behind me, I look in the mirror, my eyes already rimmed red. "Get it together, Kate," I chastise myself.

I squeeze my eyes shut. What do I know about keeping a guy around? I've never done it. My mom never did either.

Splashing water on my face, I head back out to find the waitress at our table, her hips propped suggestively against the chipped Formica as she gives a high laugh at something Luke has said.

My hands ball into fists as I consider ripping her blonde hair out in chunks when Luke senses me or something.

He's leaned back in the booth, his good arm slung along the back, rocking the casual sexy air he does so well.

In front of him is a phonebook. That's right. He asked me about that. Who does he need to call that he'd find their number in there? We're hours from Vegas…

He turns and our eyes meet.

My breath stops in my chest, as he holds out a hand toward me. I know it's his bad arm and he shouldn't be using it like that, but I heed the call anyway.

At his gesture, the waitress catches sight of me too, and she takes an involuntary step back as my hand slips into Luke's.

He pulls me down next to him and before I can question what he's doing, he gives me a long, slow kiss in front of the entire diner.

I swear, time stops as my eyes flutter closed.

When they open, the waitress is gone. Luke pushes my steaming hot cup of coffee from my side of the table to where I'm now sitting. "Drink it before it gets cold."

Without a word, I take a sip.

Ten minutes later, another waitress brings our food. Fine by me. Luke and I eat in silence, but this one doesn't trouble me a bit.

And as we get up to leave, an older woman stops me. "Keep a hold of that one," she whispers. "That is a good egg."

I smile and nod, following Luke to the counter where he pays the bill. Walking outside, he helps me up into his truck. But I don't stay on my side.

By the time he climbs in, I've already slid over to the middle.

He gives me a one-sided grin as he wraps a hand around my thigh. "You weren't jealous of that waitress, were you?"

I wince and then shrug, knowing that I'm being totally obvious.

He only shakes his head. "Kate, sweetheart. There are a million girls like that. I've only ever met one you."

"Oh," I whisper.

"I don't give Vincent Vendetti credit for much, but even he could tell you were special."

I don't know about that, but I lean my head on his shoulder anyway as we back out of the spot and start down the road.

One stop for gas and another at this town's drugstore and we're off. The windows down, we cruise along the highway.

I try to tell myself that this time, I'm just going to relax and enjoy whatever time I get with Luke Kincaid.

But my heart already aches a bit. He's going to be a tough man to let go.

CHAPTER TEN

LUKE

WE STOP midday to refuel the truck and grab some road snacks.

I love Alice, but the gas is seriously eating into the budget.

When Kate goes into pay, I pull out my burner and call Kincaid Enterprises. I get the front reception.

"Kincaid Enterprises, how may I direct your call?"

"Mason Kincaid," I answer, blowing out a long breath.

"One moment, please."

I hear the line connect. I know I won't get Mason directly, but I know all three of his assistants.

If any one of them answers…

But no one does. My brow furrows. What the fuck is that about? Instead, I go to voicemail. "This is Luke. I need Mason and I need him now. He can call me at…" Fuck. What was the burner's number?

Kate comes back out, carrying a bag of food as I hang up the phone. "Hey…" I wave the phone. "Know how I find the number to this thing?"

"Who're you calling?" she asks, tossing the snacks behind the seat and pulling out my Walmart bags, finding the box for the phone.

"My family." I hit redial and get the operator again.

"Mason Kincaid," I repeat, pulling the truck out of the spot.

I once again go to voicemail. "Hey. It's Luke again. Here is the number." Kate holds up the box. "Can you read it to me?" I ask.

She does, me repeating the numbers one at a time. "Call me ASAP."

"You think your family can help?" Kate asks as I toss the phone on the dash.

"Definitely," I answer without elaborating. My family being mega rich isn't a secret. But right now, we're in this bubble. I like it. I could have been this guy.

Maybe I should have been this guy. Beat-up pickup, worn boots, Walmart T-shirt. I would have been all right. Hell, I can still land a girl in med school even without the money. And I just get to feed her, and tinker with Alice, and…

I don't know. It feels more me than anything has for a long time.

I'm not even sure why I don't tell her about my family. Could be she'd realize I'm as bad as Vincent. That she needs a different plan besides sticking to my side.

Could be that I know the truth. She'd be safer away from me. And now that I've got a line to Mason, I'll be going back to Vegas very soon.

I don't need Kate anymore. And she needs to get back too. She's got the internship starting.

She's got her head on my shoulder, her nose periodically rubbing the fabric of my T-shirt.

Hell, I haven't gotten ahold of Mason yet. And I won't just leave Kate on some corner. I'll make sure she's tucked somewhere safe. Able to get back.

It takes up most of the day, but we finally pull off down a dirt road around nightfall. Alice doesn't go anywhere quick, and Kate insisted on hitting a grocery store so she can cook for us. Which is a good idea. We'll spend far less on groceries than on gas and eating out.

I haven't heard back from Mason, which pisses me off and honestly worries me. Is Roman all right? How much shit are they in? Should I have gone back to Vegas? Kate could have navigated...

But as we pull up to the cabin, I stop worrying and just stare.

It's absolutely fantastic.

Built with logs, it's small, but clean on the outside with a nice porch and even flower boxes.

"You're sure the guy who owns this doesn't care that we're using it?"

"Well, we've got a phone now, I can call him." Kate holds out her hand and I pass her the phone.

She fires it up and then starts to dial before she looks at me blushing. I love her cheeks all pink. "Is it all right if I tell him you're my boyfriend?"

"What?"

"I don't really know how else..." Now she's bright red. "I have to give him some explanation."

I wink, my hand settling back on her thigh as I squeeze. Does she want to play boyfriend/girlfriend? I'm going to fuck her so good tonight. "Go for it, love."

She hits the call button. "Hey, Mark," she starts, "it's Kate."

I hear the warm greeting on the other end of the phone and a bit of jealousy makes my hand tighten. "It's good to hear your voice too."

"No. I'm good. Yeah. School is going good. Thanks for the help this semester. I don't know how I would have done it if you hadn't."

My eyes go wide. This isn't just some guy she kind of knows. He helped her with tuition? Who did she say he was? My fingers flex, moving closer to her pussy because that shit is mine.

I get it. I keep pushing the possessive angle. I let out a long breath, trying to relax.

"Yeah. Mom's good. I mean, she's Mom. You know."

I watch her as she shifts in her seat. "Hey, I'm on a road trip with my boyfriend." That's right. She's passing me off as her boyfriend. This time, I really do relax back into the seat.

"Yeah. New. But I have that week off and we thought we'd get away."

"The cabin. Really? You're sure you don't mind?"

"Yeah. I remember where the key is. I'll water everything. Yeah. I remember how to start the stove."

I swallow down a lump, something so intimate in this conversation. He sounds like a nice guy. "I love you too," Kate hangs up, then quietly hands the phone back.

"Who did you say Mark was?"

"My stepdad. I mean, him and my mom got divorced after a couple years but…" Her hands knot together. "He's the only real dad I've ever had. All the others…"

"All the others?"

She dips her chin lower. "My mom dated a lot of guys. A lot of them really shitty. Twice, the guys she was with were so bad, I'd run away to Mark."

I'm fully turning in my seat. I thought I had it bad. Yeah, my dad up and left us, but my mom was rock solid. "Shit. Kate."

She shrugs. "We still talk all the time. Me and Mark. I guess I talk to him more than I do my actual mom now that I'm an adult."

She brushes at her cheek. Is she crying? I use my good arm to tug her closer. "I get it."

"Do you?"

"Mostly. My dad wasn't around either. The men in my family aren't the most dependable."

"I see." I hear the warble in her voice.

"But my mom, she raised me right. She didn't date until after Arabella left."

"Arabella?"

"My cousin. Single mom and she takes in two kids that aren't even hers. They were Kincaids, my dad's family, but she still loved them like her own."

"I'd like to meet your mom."

I smile at her. "Yeah. She's a good woman."

Kate slides away from me on the bench seat. "Want to go inside? We've got a lot of unpacking to do."

"Sure. This place is amazing."

"It's tiny, but really just as cute on the inside as it is on the outside. I remember when Mark built it. He let me pick all the furniture and the curtains. My mom hated it here, but I've always loved it."

I get why.

She opens her door and hops out of the truck. I get out too and come around to her side. "You know. This place matches your truck well. A little dingy but in the best kind of way with all kinds of charm."

"My favorite," I answer, pushing the seat forward to get the bags in the back. Bright side. No one is finding us here.

Mason can take all the time he wants to call me back. Well, as long as it's in the next twenty-four hours.

The permits expire in like three more days and I need to make sure my family comes out on top of this one if we're ever going to get rid of the Vendettis.

Still, at least for tonight, I'm treating this like an actual vacation. I've got a beautiful woman by my side, tucked in the pine trees of Colorado. What could be better?

But an hour later, it is.

Because Kate starts cooking, her ass looking amazing in her jeans as I sit at the retro table, the kitchen filling with the most amazing smells.

I'd gotten a six-pack of beer at the grocery store and I crack one open now, taking a swig.

Kate turns around, and seeing the open bottle, steps away from the stove, picking it up and taking a swig too.

We're at the sharing-drinks phase, are we?

This is all new territory for me, but I hook her waist, pulling her close and plant a kiss on her belly. Her shirt has a bit of a crop so just enough of her skin is exposed that I plant my lips on it, tasting her.

She swats lightly at my shoulder and then returns to the stove. I prop a foot on the other chair, leaning back. I can't remember the last time I was this relaxed.

That's when I hear a scratching right outside the door.

"Fuck," I'm on my feet in a second, Kate freezes at the stove.

Grabbing a knife from the block, I start toward the front door.

CHAPTER ELEVEN

KATE

I TURN OFF THE STOVE, not wanting to burn the place down. Mark would be devastated…

My breath catches as Luke turns off the lights and then creeps to the front door.

The woods are full of all kinds of interesting creaks and groans, but this was definitely scratching, and it was definitely on the porch.

Luke slides the door open, the wood only making the slightest squeak as he pokes his head out.

"Argh," he growls out and then I hear it, the skittering of little feet.

"What was it?" I gasp, my hand coming to my throat.

He closes the door, flipping the light back on. "Raccoon looking for a handout."

I give the smallest laugh on a long breath of air. I should have known.

Flipping the stove back on, I finish dinner, just a simple stir fry. Our diet has been short of vegetables, though, and I could use some.

"Things to know about the cabin," I say as I plate. "It has a very small well for water, so we have a running toilet and fresh, drinkable water in the sinks, but there isn't enough pressure for a shower so…"

"So?"

"We bathe in the creek."

I set the plates down in front of him. He lifts his fork but waits for me to sit too. "Fine by me as long as we're bathing together."

I sit down, picking up my fork too. For a guy that told me he doesn't do relationships, he sure does do intimacy. From that little show for the waitress, to the way he's always touching me, I've never felt more… wanted.

"You know," I lean forward, nipping at my lip. "The best time for a bath is at night."

He leans forward too. "I like where your head's at."

I grin, my chin dipping as I look down at my plate. Dropping my fork, I scoop up some stir fry, taking a bite. Glancing up at Luke through my lashes, I try to keep my heart from racing.

He's just so much man. He sits at the table, eating the dinner I made for him, arms flexing. "This is delicious, Kate. Thank you."

I don't mean to, but in my head, we start playing house.

Like me cooking for him, spending every night wrapped up in his arms. But I'm in med school. I have this whole plan for a career, and it was never supposed to involve a guy.

But right about now…

"You know, I'm not a bad cook either. I'll cook for you tomorrow night."

Even better.

We finish eating, and Luke gets up, clearing my plate and washing the dishes. No dishwasher here.

I lean back in my chair, just watching him work. I swear, I could fall for this guy. Fall hard.

THE ONLY TIME I've ever been in love was when I was getting my biology degree at NYU. I fell head over heels, but unlike with Luke, I waited to have sex because I wanted it to be really special.

Found him in bed with my roommate one night. That one was fun.

There is no way that Luke is the guy who doesn't break my heart.

"Watcha thinkin' back there, kitten?"

I roll my eyes. "Kitten? Please."

He drains the sink, drying his hands. "You've been quiet tonight."

"Have I?" I shrug. "Being here is stirring old feelings, I guess." New ones too. "I told you, Mark was one of the really good guys."

"What happened? Between him and your mom?"

I shrug. "I think she got bored. But she ended up going on a bender in Reno. Found a new guy, who didn't last long, but he stuck long enough that she dumped Mark. When she and the new guy burned out, I made her move back to Colorado. It's the only place I was ever happy. And even though she left Mark…"

"You didn't."

I shook my head. "There was one guy she dated while I was in high school…" I stop, looking away. I don't want to tell this story and I'm sorry I started it. I'm not sure what's gotten into me tonight.

Luke squats down in front of me, taking my hands in his. "Kate."

No *kitten*. No *love*. My throat burns. "Sorry. We don't have to do this, actually."

He lets go of my hands and slides his palms over my legs until he's holding my hips. "If you tell me, I'll tell you one of my secrets."

I feel tears burning my eyes. Part of me wants to get it out. I didn't even tell my mom or Mark what actually happened. I just refused to go home with her as long as that guy was in the house. Him or me… She capitulated when Mark backed me up.

"I think what that makes it hard to tell anyone is that there is a piece of me that worries what happened was my fault."

"Baby girl," he whispers, leaning forward to plant a kiss into the crown of my hair. "I know it wasn't your fault. So why don't you tell me?"

"My mom was gone for three days, probably on a bender. She did that a lot. And her boyfriend of the time, he got more and more restless. I…" I swallow. "One day when I got home from school, he just…"

"What did he do?" His voice is so soft, so soothing, I almost miss the steel underneath it.

"He pinned me to a wall," I curl down until my face is in the crook of his neck. "Touched me a lot of places that I..."

"How'd you get away?"

"I broke a vase over his head and knocked him out."

"Good girl," Luke brushes my hair back from my face, stroking his fingers through the strands. His touch is so gentle, his gaze unreadable. "What happened next?"

"I got the hell out of there. Ran to Mark. I told him enough that when my mom finally came back, he threatened to call the state unless she kicked the guy out."

"What was the guy's name?"

"It doesn't matter now."

"Tell me anyway, sweetheart."

"Chris Stanton."

"Chris Stanton," he repeats like he's trying to memorize it. "Chris Stanton."

"Like I said. Part of me has always worried—"

"It wasn't your fault."

I shake my head. "I said yes to Vincent Vendetti when he asked me out. Maybe I just attract..."

"There are a lot of terrible people out there, Kate. Running into a few of them isn't a reflection on you."

Maybe. Maybe not. I am my mother's daughter.

"Tell me yours now."

He draws in a deep breath, a grimace crossing his face. "I... uh... I can't read so well."

My brows draw together. "What?"

He shrugs. "I graduated high school. But I struggle to remember numbers, order words on paper. You know how I had you read me the number on the burner? Navigate the signs out of Vegas? I mix shit up in my head."

I blink up at him. He's so confident. Strong. "But that's okay. Your job is probably perfect for you and—"

"My job?" he looks at me with confusion.

"Construction?"

His eyes widen in surprise before a look crosses his face like he's in pain. He runs a hand through his hair. "Love, I don't operate a bulldozer."

"What do you do then?"

"I'm more of a project manager." A muscle in his jaw tics and my brows draw together as I try to understand. "Though I've been struggling with the job."

"But you're gainfully employed?" I nip at my lip knowing that I'm giving my own fears away. Bum magnet at your service.

"Gainfully employed? Yeah. I'm employed."

I let out a long, relieved breath. "Thank goodness."

He gives me a smile, reaching for my face too, and gives me a long slow kiss. "So you're worried that you…"

"Attract the wrong kind of guy," I shrug, laying it out there. "And you're worried that you're not smart enough?"

"And that I'm drafting off my family. You know?"

I shake my head. "If I were to guess, they think about you the way I do. There isn't anyone I'd rather have by my side when trouble comes knocking."

The small smile on his lips spreads, making him toe-curling gorgeous. "Thanks for that, love."

I draw in a deep breath. "I know this thing with us is convenient and temporary…"

His smile slips. "Okay."

"But I just want you to know that I think you're a Mark." I need him to understand. Even when things end…

"A Mark?"

"A guy that I can count on. You know?"

"Kate, you have trouble anytime, anywhere, you call me." And then he kisses me. There is no tongue, but somehow, there is so much feeling in it. Like we're sealing some pact.

I cling to him as he kisses me over and over, finally opening my lips and he brushes his tongue against mine. He pulls me down off the chair, until I'm sitting in his lap, both of us on the floor.

This kiss is different. It's tender, it's warm. The heat is slower to unfurl but I've never felt safer than I do in his arms right now.

I wonder what I'd give to stay here. I'd guess almost anything.

He starts to get up, pulling me with him. "Your arm," I cry out as he lifts me up.

"Starting to feel better," he answers before he captures my mouth again. "And just so we're clear, we're taking that bath and we're taking the time to strip naked first. No clothes tonight."

I should have known he was successful. He's got this way of telling me what to do that brokers no argument. "What else?" I say, the heat instantly turning up.

"You promised to suck my cock."

"I did."

"And I'm going to eat you out until you scream my name. No one around here to be quiet for."

Did I say the heat was building slowly?

I'm soaked in a second and so ready for whatever he wants to do.

CHAPTER TWELVE

KATE

LUKE CARRIES me outside into the night. I have one moment where I wonder if this is a good idea. We did have an unwanted visitor.

But then, he kisses me again and I forget to worry. He makes it down the embankment without a misstep, which is impressive. I have trouble with the steep bank in the best of circumstances.

But I don't get a chance to say this as his mouth devours mine.

Finally, he sets me down on my bare feet, which splash in the water, getting the bottom of my jeans wet.

"Clothes off," he rumbles, not leaving much room for arguing. Not that I would have. I peel off my shirt and unhook my bra, tossing them both on the bank.

He pulls me against his front, bending low to suck one of my nipples into his mouth. "This is how we end up with clothing still on," I gasp out, arching my back to give him more access. His mouth feels so good, I scrape my fingers over his scalp, pulling him closer.

He swirls his tongue over the stiff peak before he lifts his head. "You're right. The rest of the clothes off. I want to see you naked."

It's crazy that we never quite make it to that point. I've had something on both times we've done it. I strip the jeans over my hips, nearly falling as I try to get the wet bottoms over my feet.

He shoots out a hand to steady me.

I just get the second leg off my foot when I shoot him a glare. "You're still dressed."

"Let me look at you for a second," he grunts as his hands come out to trace my slender hips.

I feel myself blushing. Thank goodness for the dark, but I still have to resist the urge to cover up. I literally had my ass in the air for this guy last night. But this is different.

It's not quite the heat of passion, and I'm well aware that Luke can have any woman he wants.

His hands continue down my legs and then over my ass, tracing the curve of my back. "So pretty."

I shake my head. "I've always hated that."

"What? Being pretty?"

"Pretty gets a pat on the head. Beautiful wins the prize." Christ, every insecurity I have is coming out tonight.

He strips off his shirt then, tossing it on top of my stuff. Then he shucks off his jeans with a lot more grace than I did. Naked, he bends down wrapping his arms under my ass as he lifts me in his arms.

I hold onto his neck, curling my body around him.

"I've never met a woman who was so perfectly pretty," he rumbles against my belly. "It's your hands. Your arms. The way your brows arch. Hell, even your feet are adorable."

I snort. "Adorable is worse than pretty."

He laughs into my skin. "Maybe you're right in general. But not about me. I've never wanted to wrap a woman up more than I do you."

"It's probably because when we met, I had a gun to my head."

"Don't fucking remind me," he rumbles, his arms tightening. "I'd never let Vendetti hurt you, though, love."

"Thank you," I whisper.

"And I do think you're beautiful," he says kissing my belly button.

"There is just something so vulnerable about your looks, I can't help but want to tuck you away where you're safe and warm."

I arch my head back, the words shivering through me. I want him to keep me safe and warm. God, I just want him.

He lays me down on a high, flat rock that's out of the water, and, as if to prove his point, he starts kissing every part of me.

It's not just my stomach or my breasts. He kisses down my arms, planting a kiss on each of my palms. He kisses each fingertip.

Then he moves to my hip, trailing his lips down my leg until he reaches my foot. I barely keep from giggling when he nips at the arch of my foot. But then when he sucks each of my toes into his mouth...

"Luke," I gasp out as he grazes his teeth over my pinky toe. "That is..."

"You're delicious," he rumbles as starts licking and nipping up the inside of my leg. "I want to devour every part of you."

He nips the inside of my knee and then starts nibbling up my thigh. I flex my hips, the ache of need making me uncomfortable. I crave the friction I know he'll give. "I want you to devour me."

He stops on the inside of my thigh. "Don't doubt your appeal, Kate. Everything about you makes me crazy. It's the way you move, smell, touch. It's your reaction to me."

He holds my hips in his hands and then dives into my pussy, licking me exactly where I needed it.

I cry out, scraping my back on the rock as I arch closer.

He eats me like he's starving and I'm oblivious to everything but his tongue. I shift again, wanting more.

But he stops. I lift my head with a cry of protest. "Don't stop."

But he's pushing out of the water, climbing onto the rock. "Your skin," he rumbles.

My brow furrows. I don't even know what he means for a moment. Then I realize he's talking about my back. "It's fine."

But in a series of a few quick moves, I'm on top of him, his back on the rock.

Somehow, he spins me so that my pussy is in his face, his cock in mine. "Oh," I breathe as I flick my tongue out and take a good long lick.

He rumbles into my folds and then flattens his tongue to lick every part of me at once.

I moan, my eyes closing for a second it's so good.

When I open them, I can see a pearl of cum right on the tip of his cock, glistening in the moonlight.

I lick him again, collecting the salty liquid on my tongue.

"Woman," he growls into my sensitive skin. "Wrap your lips around me before I explode."

For some reason, his command only make me hotter, and I slide my lips over the tip, taking more and more of him between my lips and into the heat of my mouth.

He groans right into me, and then starts working my clit with his tongue, his finger sliding into my pussy.

It feels so good I'm deep-throating him as I chase my own orgasm, our bodies climbing together.

It's one time I could have been as loud as I wanted, but I can hardly make a noise, my mouth is so full.

It doesn't stop me from cumming though, my body spasming as a powerful orgasm rips through me.

Luke isn't done with me. Rolling me to the side, he's got his arms around me, pulling me into the water with him.

I wrap my legs around his waist even as he thrusts into my now-sopping pussy. "Fuck, sweetheart, you feel so fucking good."

He's standing in thigh high water, supporting my weight as he pulls my hips up and then pulls me back down on his cock.

My head snaps back, my back arching as I let out a low moan. His arm must be feeling better, but it can't be a hundred percent. I have this moment where I wonder what sex will be like when it is.

It only makes me hotter. He's pumping in and out of me, grinding our bodies together as I hold on for dear life.

His mouth finds mine, his tongue thrusting between my lips as another orgasm tightens every muscle in my body.

Finally, I can't take any more and I break apart, screaming into his mouth.

It triggers his orgasm, his thrusts so rapid, he rattles my teeth as he cums too. He's still cumming when he sinks down into the water, dropping to his knees so that the water is up to our chests.

I've still got my arms wound around his neck and his chin sinks onto my shoulder, my cheek coming to his temple.

"That was…"

"I know," he says, squeezing me tightly.

I take in several deep breaths, letting the cool water soothe my overheated skin.

A muffled ring calls out into the night, and I turn my head. Is that a phone?

His hands spread out on my back. "We've only got one issue."

A bit of fear slides down my spine as I lift my head, pulling his up by his hair to look in his eyes. "What?"

"Mason's calling me and once I pick up, we're going back to Vegas."

CHAPTER THIRTEEN

LUKE

"VEGAS," she says it on a sigh. Like it makes her sad, but relieved too. We both need to go back. Me for the sake of my family, her for the big career she has planned.

Gently, I wade toward the shore, the phone stops its incessant ring. I fully stand, setting her on the ground just as it starts again.

Picking up my pants, I pull out the phone and accept the call. "Hello?"

"Thank fucking God," Mason rumbles in my ear. I don't want to worry about pleasantries now though.

"Roman? He good?"

"Good," Mason answers.

I nearly wilt to the ground. "How?"

"The vision-impaired girl. She brought him in. Helped him escape." He isn't the only man who got a meaningful assist from a woman.

I turn to Kate as she gasps.

"Maddie?" I ask. But it reminds me I have an audience. Pulling the microphone away from my mouth I lean in and kiss her lips.

"She's fine. And Roman too," Mason says.

Still naked, I work my way up the bank in three quick jumps.

"The permits?"

He clears his throat. "We're working on them."

I run a hand through my hair and then turn my head to the side, cracking my neck. That is a fucking relief that Mason is cleaning up my mess. Then again, what's new? "What do you need from me?"

"Guerriero? Is he on your tail?"

"Pretty sure I lost Gorilla yesterday. Now we're in the middle of nowhere, at a family friend's cabin in southern Colorado that no one can trace to either of us."

Mason laughs, sounding relieved. "You always were a scrappy fuck. But let me just double check one detail. Who is the other person in the *we* you just mentioned?"

Mason never misses a detail. "Name's Kate."

"Vincent's date."

"How the fuck do you know that?"

"Maddie. The vision-impaired girl." He says, like he's busy thinking other things. "I hear Kate's in med school. She patch you up all right?"

"Fit as a fiddle."

"Good. So no additional medical care required?" I look at the phone for a second before I answer.

"No. Our biggest problem is being short on money. And time."

"I can wire you some," Mason says. "No problem."

"I've got enough to get back to Vegas." My muscles are twitching, ready for action. "Unless you can send the helicopter?"

Mason is silent, not answering my question. "You really think that you lost him? Gorilla?"

"Yeah."

"In that case, I might want you to stay put."

"What?" I rumble into the phone.

Kate is slowly picking her way up the bank. I take a step toward her and reach out my hand to her, pulling her up. As soon as she's on solid ground, I'm making my way to the porch. I don't know what Mason's got in mind, but Kate can't stay here at the cabin.

"We raided the Vendettis' house and they're under arrest."

I stop again, halfway up the porch. "Are you fucking serious?"

"Suspected murder," he whispers into the phone. "Of you."

"Shit."

"You can't just resurface, not now, Luke. You being gone… that gives us a unique opportunity. If I can keep them in prison, at least until I clear the permits, then we'll be able to clean up this mess."

Fuck. Fuck. Fuck. I see the problem. I need to do this for my family. I fuck up so much. This is the one time they need me. "All right, but Kate's got to go back tomorrow."

Mason cuts me off. "She can't, Luke."

I grimace, staring at the phone. "Why not?"

"Think about it. One, she'd be in danger. Two, if they find her and question her, she'd give away the whole ruse. It's best if she stays with you."

My gut twists into knots.

I have to do this for Mason. I should say no for Kate.

Her skin glows in the moonlight as she makes her way to me. Maybe it's not so bad.

It's just a summer internship.

"Mason. I can't fuck with her life like that."

"You're not fucking with her life. The Vendettis did that."

He's not wrong but still… "I like her. She's—"

"Safest with you." Mason cuts me off. "Luke. I'll try my damnedest to push the permits through tomorrow. But if I don't… There is no choice here. We need to keep the Vendettis in jail for everyone's safety and I need you to stay put. Please."

I let out a long breath. I can't say no. "All right. We'll stay."

"Thank you," Mason lets out a long breath. "Are you near the San Juan National Forest?"

"Yeah."

"There is a bank I can wire money to in Durango. It's close enough for you to drive but far enough away…"

"No one will find us." I run a hand through my hair as Kate comes up the steps.

We're both naked and I turn, pulling her against me. She's cold, and wrapping an arm around her middle, I pull her close, pressing her skin to mine as I drop a kiss on her shoulder. She nuzzles into my chest as guilt eats at my stomach.

She's the last person I want to hurt.

Part of me was worried it would come to this. Maybe that's why I never told her who I am. What my family does.

We are a giant Vegas machine, and we crush everyone who gets in our way.

Even beautiful little doctors with shiny brown hair and soulful eyes.

"I'll have the package for you first thing tomorrow morning," Mason says. "I'm glad you're safe."

"Yeah," I say and then I hang up, my other arm wrapping around Kate. Was she worried about being with a bad guy?

I might be the worst. "We should get some sleep," I murmur into her shoulder. "I've got to head out early tomorrow morning."

"For what?"

"My family is wiring us money."

"We're not going back to Vegas tomorrow?" She stiffens in my arms, her breath catching.

The lie I'm about to tell sits bitter on my tongue. "The Italians are turning Vegas upside down looking for us."

She cries out, pulling back. "But… my internship!"

"I'm sorry, Kate. I don't think it's safe."

She shakes her head, her hair brushing all over my skin. "But, Luke, you don't understand. This is my chance. I've waited forever. Beat out thousands of candidates. I can't not show up on the first day!"

My eyes close. "Baby girl…"

I hear the soft sob, and I know she's crying. I tighten my grip, crushing her against my chest, wanting to take the words back. Wanting to promise to drive her back to the city tomorrow. I want to promise her the world. Instead, I hold my tongue.

Because I owe Mason everything.

So instead, I just let her cry out her tears into my shoulder as they soak my skin. I run my hand over her hair, settling my hand over the small of her back. I'm going to hell.

I've heard everything she's said about her mother. The string of men. I know what she's trying to escape. The life she's attempting to build for herself that will bury her past hurts deep.

We understand each other.

I don't think I've felt that kind of connection with another person for a very long time.

I've been trying to escape myself too. The man who can barely read. The least valuable cog in the Kincaid wheel. Only, there is no easy way out of this.

And Kate… she's not escaping herself either. A date with one bum, Vincent Vendetti, a ride with another—me—and her future is about to be crushed.

CHAPTER FOURTEEN

KATE

I WAKE up to the bed moving, Luke climbing out. He's still naked, but so am I for that matter.

Not that we'd done much more than fall asleep after we collapsed into bed. After I'd cried out every tear in my body.

My eyes are scratchy and I'm sure they're red and puffy. I stretch sitting up. "You're leaving already?"

"No, love. Bank doesn't open until nine. I just can't sleep."

His words wake me up. Is something wrong? I hope not. I've never felt more connected to another person.

I let the blankets fall, skimming down my body and let them pool around my waist. "Want to go for a swim?"

His eyes trail down my naked body, heating with every second that passes. "You sure you want to do that? You were upset last night…"

I sigh as I push up onto my knees, giving a good stretch, arms over my head, as the blankets remain on the bed.

I watch his cock swell. How is it that we've been naked together for hours and it doesn't feel weird?

His reaction only excites me, and I twist my hair up, my arms over my head, arching my back.

I was incredibly sad last night. But here's the thing: the guy who held me while I cried, kissed my forehead and murmured words of encouragement, is currently staring at me like I'm the most desirable thing he's ever seen.

Did I think Luke Kincaid might be a bum?

He's a gem.

Gorgeous, charismatic, kind to strangers and children, protective of me. I want Luke inside me right now.

He steps up behind me, his hand coming to the hair I'm holding up with my fingers as he pulls my hands away.

My hair falls down like a curtain, streaming down my back. It's long, reaching my midback, and he twists the strands around his hand like a rope, pulling it the slightest bit. "Sweetheart," he murmurs into my exposed neck. "I'm a little feral this morning. And you had a rough night."

"I want your feral." I can already feel myself getting slick.

And it's true. It's like the nicer that Luke is, the dirtier I become. He pulls my hair harder, really tipping my head back even further.

I guess we're not making it to the river.

I only wanted to go to soak my face and get rid of the puffiness.

But it's a moot point as Luke ceases pulling and starts pushing, sending me to my hands and knees on the bed. I go willingly, heating even more when he nudges my knees apart.

His other hand comes between my legs, sliding up my slit, rubbing me until I'm like a cat, chasing his touch.

I'm about to beg him to put his cock inside me, when he uses his hips to nudge me the rest of the way down onto my belly, before he flips me over onto my back and then plunges inside me.

No wonder this position is so popular. When he bottoms out inside me, he's pushing every button I have and I gasp in a breath, wrapping my arms around his neck and arching into his body.

He feels so good. "Luke," I gasp. "Just like that. Oh God."

"Scream it out, love. Scream it loud." And he starts fucking me with long, hard thrusts that have the bed shaking.

We could wake the dead with the noise we're making. Fortunately, there aren't many living people around as I scream his name.

He's got both his arms around me, holding me close as he ratchets up the pace. My body is humming, on fire, as I thread my fingers in his hair, biting into his shoulder. He tastes so good, I close my eyes as my insides explode with an orgasm.

It's hard and fast and so perfect, I scream again, my legs locking around his hips.

He roars too, his movements losing all their finesse as he cums. I hold him close as he empties inside me, and I keep my arms around him for the longest time after he's done.

Sex with Luke, time with this man, is a pretty sweet consolation prize, if I'm losing my internship.

Maybe it's a sign, I wasn't meant to be a surgeon. I'm not even sure it's what I really wanted. It was about the money. About the prestige. About proving to the world I could be whatever I wanted.

But what do I want?

I haven't stepped out of my world for the longest time, and now that I'm here, it's a good time to ask.

Luke finally lifts up, sliding to the side and resting on one elbow. He trails his fingers down the middle of my torso his eyes following. "You're so perfect."

I shake my head. How is that he thinks that? I roll too, pressing my front to his. "Me?"

He trails kisses over my hair. "Don't even try to say I'm perfect. We both know I'm not."

"I like you just the way you are," I whisper into his neck.

But the words only push him off the bed. What did I say?

"How about that swim?" he rumbles before he turns and scoops me up into his arms.

"Your arm," I gasp, my hands going around his neck.

"Arm is fine, nearly all better," he says, striding through the cabin and out the front door.

"That cannot be true," I gasp out as he jostles me down the front porch stairs. "I have expert knowledge that you're lying."

He chuckles. "I don't mind a bit of pain as long as everything works."

He crosses the yard and then moves down the bank like he's not carrying an entire person. I let out a little yelp, half in fear, half in excitement.

Luke splashes into the water and when he's thigh high, sinks down under the surface, me still in his arms.

I gasp as the cool water hits my skin, clutching him and his warmth closer. He only laughs harder. "Ready to go under?"

I let out a giggle and then he mock dips me, like he's prepping me for the plunge. Closing my eyes, I hold my breath and then we're going under, the cool water feels amazing on my still-puffy face.

We surface again, my mock shrieks of protest echoing through the quiet of the morning. He laughs too, but quiets first.

Stifling my own giggles, I look up at him. Our eyes hold for a second, two before he drops his mouth to mine. "Maybe we'll make it back to Vegas tonight. Maybe my family will…"

I shake my head. "I'm calling the lead surgeon today to ask for a late start. I can't take the chance of calling tomorrow, when he's expecting me to arrive. It'll be worse if I do."

I see Luke wince, but he gives a single stiff nod.

Pushing out of his arms, I move to the shore where we left the shampoo, conditioner, and soap last night. Dipping my head back under, I squirt shampoo into my hand and start lathering, soaping up the long strands.

I catch Luke watching over my shoulder, his body still dipped down in the water up to his chest.

His eyes are dark and heavy, but I catch something new in their depths. Regret? Worry?

I sink under the water, rinsing out my hair, before I surface again and grab the conditioner. "Everything all right?"

"It's fine," he gives me a perfunctory smile and then pushes to the shore as well, shampooing his own hair.

He stands on the shore, his back to me, his body on full display in the early morning light, muscles flexing.

He's so gorgeous, it's almost hard to breathe. I wash my body while he's facing away, and then dive back in the water to rinse.

I'm still under swimming when his body glides under mine, pushing me up to the surface.

"Luke," I gasp when we both break the water. "What are you doing?"

His arms go around me as he plants his feet on the bottom. My legs naturally come around him which has his cock pressing into my folds. "Your ass was the only thing out of the water, and it was fantastic."

I shake my head, but any chastisement I might have issued is forgotten as he sinks into my pussy. I instantly tighten around him, my head falling back. "I just got clean," I murmur, shifting to take more of him in.

His hand comes to the top of my ass, pushing me all the way down his cock until he bottoms out. "I can't get enough," he rumbles into my shoulder.

My arms come around his neck, like I'm holding on for dear life. I can't get enough either.

Which isn't surprising. Luke is hands down the hottest man I've ever met or even seen. And that includes models on posters and actors on television.

He can't think the same thing about me. His other hand splays out on my back, his mouth kissing a trail up my neck as he holds deep inside me.

"I'm not going anywhere," I reassure, some deep part of me sensing that he's both more distant and more desperate to be close. Is this about the call? Did speaking to his family upset him?

Did my crying make him worried?

"Luke," I run my hands down his back. "It's all right if I don't make it back tomorrow."

"What?"

I lean back too, which, amazingly, pushes him even deeper inside me. My eyes widen as I nearly lose the words.

"It's not okay, love. Not at all."

I shake my head. "A new opportunity will come up. A better one. I'll end up where I'm supposed to be."

I see the pain flash across his face a moment before he pulls me close again, lifting my hips to plunge back inside me.

I forget anything else I wanted to say as he picks up the pace, my passion, his dominance taking me over.

I've never wanted anything more.

CHAPTER FIFTEEN

KATE

"ALMOST DONE?" Luke calls over the roar of the blow dryer. The thing is old, from my middle school days, and not very powerful despite being loud.

But I don't want to go into town with Luke looking like I stepped out of the river while he rocks some effortless GQ look with a working-guy twist.

It makes me feel so inferior.

Maybe I can pick up an eyeliner or something today. Maybe a little gloss for my lips would be nice.

I turn off the blow dryer, assessing my hair. At least I got the loose waves right. They look soft and silky, waving back from my face.

I tug at my Walmart T-shirt as it stretches across my chest. "Ready," I call back and then open the door.

He's leaning against the wall of the kitchen, one brow quirked up as he takes me in.

I nip at my lip. "I didn't want to look like I'd been dragged through mud today."

"You always look beautiful," he rumbles. "But that hair looks so gorgeous all blown out, I can't wait to mess it up."

My cheeks flush as I look down with a smile. Now that he's said it, that's exactly what I was hoping for.

His hand loops around my waist, brushing the bare skin between my shirt and my shorts as he pulls me outside.

He helps me into the truck and then fires her up, turning the truck around to head down the long dirt road that passes as a driveway.

We finally pull onto the road and start the hour-long drive to Durango. In a different car it would be shorter, but Alice won't go over forty-five.

Fine by me. With the wind filling the cabin, I lounge back in my seat, wondering where I'm headed next.

We finally reach Durango and pull into the bank. "Can I make a call while you're in there?" It's just nine, the bank doors opening. If I call now, I might be able to catch the doctor before his first procedure.

"Sure," he tosses me the burner. "Good luck."

I catch his grimace. Is he nervous for me? I appreciate it, but I'm pretty resigned at this point. He'll either give me the extension or he'll take away the position.

With trembling fingers, I dial the number, having called enough times, it comes easily.

It rings twice and the doctor's assistant picks up. "Doctor Shrewsbury's office."

"Karen," I say warmly. We've talked a lot over the last several months. "It's Kate. Is Doctor Shrewsbury available."

"Kate," she gushes. "You're just in time. I'll put you through."

I draw in a cleansing breath as the line rings again.

"Kate?" Dr. Shrewsbury picks up. "How are you?"

"Good," I answer, wincing. "You?"

"Wondering why you might be calling."

He's a cut-through-the-bullshit kind of guy.

"Yes. Of course. I went on a hiking trip, explore-the-area kind of thing, and my friend's truck broke down."

"You're not calling me to pick you up?"

"No. No. I would never. But the truck needs repairs and it's going to take us an extra day or two to return to Vegas and..."

"I beg your pardon?"

His tone could cut glass. "My apologies, Doctor Shrewsbury. I'm just as committed. I just—"

"Kate. There are hundreds of students who would kill for this internship."

"I know. I'm thrilled to be working for you."

"You are no longer working for me."

I wince, my hand coming to cover my face. "Doctor Shrewsbury, please. If there was any way I could make this up, I can assure you—"

"You should never have to make up opportunities like this," he cuts me off. "You should just be here. You have proven yourself unworthy of the opportunity before it's even begun."

"Unworthy..." I repeat the word, choking on it. I'd resigned myself to losing this chance. I knew Dr. Shrewsbury was not a compromising man. But that word is like sticking a hot poker in my eye. "No one has worked harder than me—"

"I beg to differ. Every other candidate I interviewed would have made their first day of work. You were always a risk, your undergraduate degree from the University of Massachusetts, your personal credentials non-existent. I should have known better."

He keeps talking but I only catch clips of it as I sink down in the bench, my eyes welling with tears again.

It's not the missed opportunity. He's saying everything I worry is true about myself. I hold the phone away from my ear, still able to hear but at least his words are not ringing so loudly.

I don't even see Luke come up to his open window of the truck, all I can hear are the words "tactless and lazy" coming through the phone as I pull it even further away from my left ear.

Suddenly the phone is gone from my hand, Luke, reaches past the steering wheel and snatches it from my hand through the open window.

"Luke," I gasp, sitting up in my seat.

"Hello," Luke barks into the line.

"Who is this?" Dr. Shrewsbury demands.

"Luke Kincaid. Who is this?"

The line goes very quiet. I blink in surprise trying to understand as Luke walks away, his voice is low and with the whir of other cars pulling into the parking lot I don't hear what he says. I scoot across the bench seat and open his door, intent on following but he's already hanging up and turning back around. He stops just in front of me, his face taut with anger in a way that I don't even remember seeing on that first night.

"Luke?"

He grabs behind my knee, pulling me further out on the bench as he wraps his arms around me. My legs naturally settle on either side of his hips, my arms around his chest.

I hug him back, well aware we're making quite the spectacle.

"I'm sorry that asshole talked to you like that."

"It's all right," I answer, shaking my head. "I'm used to it."

He leans back, his lip curling. "That's complete bullshit."

I blink in surprise. "I'm sorry you think that, but it's kind of the way it goes when you're the one who needs someone to take a chance on you."

He softens then. "Not you, kitten. Him. He doesn't want to hire you anymore, fine. But he was a dick about it."

"Is that what you said to him?" I really like Luke and his take-charge attitude, but this is my career. It's bad enough I didn't show. The last thing I need is Luke making the good doctor mad enough that he calls my advisor and tells him that I'm difficult. That would really mess up my chances.

"No. I told him that he needed to give my wife an extension or he'd answer to me."

My mouth drops open. Which one of those phrases to unwrap first?

"Wife?"

"Men respond to that kind of claim."

"And why would he worry about answering to you?"

"I got that big dick energy. He'll let you start next week."

Now, not only is my mouth open, but I'm speechless. That can't be true…

But Luke is already sliding me across the seat, as he climbs in the truck. "Let's get a few more days' worth of groceries, just in case we don't leave tomorrow." Luke gives me his most charming smile. "I've got a few more errands to run. Can I drop you at the grocery store?"

"Luke… how…"

But he's already backing out the truck from the parking spot. He hits the gas and takes a left, pulling into a high-end grocery store. Durango has all sorts of outdoor sport adventure companies. White-water rafting, fly-fishing, hiking, just to name a few. But it also seems to have some swanky boutique places. Probably for all the rich people who come here to vacation.

I barely have time to look at fancy stores, or the people coming out of them though, as Luke shoves some cash in my hand. "Get canned goods in case we're leaving them, but get us some fresh stuff for the next few days as well? Something nice, okay?"

"All right," I answer, with a shake of my head, pocketing the money and closing the door. "Where are you going?"

I sound like a broken, needy record.

"Just down the street. I'll be back in forty-five minutes, an hour tops."

"Sure," I answer with a nod. I guess I could use a few minutes to sift through some of my feelings too.

I climb out of the truck, closing the door behind me.

I don't know if I even want the position with Dr. Shrewsbury. But how did Luke…

He's already backing out of the spot. I only watch him for a second before I head into the store.

Instantly, I stop. They have some of the most gorgeous fruit. The kind I can never afford.

I pull the cash back out and realize that Luke hit me with three one-hundred-dollar bills. How much food did he want me to buy?

I shove them back in my pocket and grab a container of strawberries.

I thought I understood Luke perfectly. He looks good in his beat-up boots and his old truck. He steals cars but he beats up criminals and helps strangers. Like he did me.

Yeah, he's a little gray, but he's got a great heart.

Then again… he stopped the doctor with the biggest chip on his shoulder in his tracks.

He hands me hundreds like it's nothing. I grab a mango, thinking of a Thai recipe that I made once and loved. If only I had a phone to look it up.

Or, I could buy a sharp cheese maybe. A charcuterie night?

I try to concentrate on the groceries, but my thoughts keep wandering. I'm only on the third aisle, when the hair stands up on the back of my neck.

Turning, I look all around me.

I don't see anything.

But that breaks my trance of wandering thoughts. I'm all business as I move through the rest of the store.

I see some wine, but I'd probably need an ID so I skip it. Instead, I make my way to the register, checking out, and then outside, where I find Luke's truck already waiting.

He gets out and helps me put the stuff in the back and then he hands me in, closing my door behind me.

I'm quiet as we make our way back out of Durango and toward the cabin.

"Everything okay?" he asks, his hand coming to my thigh.

I give him a weak smile. "Good."

"What's wrong?"

"I had the weirdest feeling in the grocery store. Like someone was watching me."

His eyes immediately go to the rearview.

Now he's quiet too and as we drive, he spends more of his time looking behind than he does ahead.

"You buckled?" he asks.

"Of course."

Suddenly, he takes a hard right, turning into a random dirt road that's heavily treed, cutting the engine.

His eyes are on the rearview.

We sit there for ten minutes, silence falling between us.

I know what he's doing. I don't need to ask. He wants to know if we've been followed.

Finally, he seems satisfied that we're not, and slowly backs out of the drive, continuing down the road.

"I didn't mean to scare you," I say as quietly as I can with the windows open.

He gives me an easy smile. Reaching for my thigh. "Never worry about telling me something that's bothering you, love."

I let out a breath, grabbing his hand in mine.

There is a lot I'm still figuring out, but I know when this man touches me, I've never felt more grounded.

CHAPTER SIXTEEN

Luke

Kate cooks dinner, but man, she's been quiet all afternoon. After talking to her boss, I felt miles better. I had solved the problem my family and our business had created.

I could make love to her again, and not feel like a complete fraud. And yeah, I'm fucking aware I just said the words *make love* instead of just calling it fucking. But that's how it feels with Kate.

Like I'm making love. When I'm inside her with her arms around me, her eyes on me, there is a connection between us I've never felt before.

Maybe it's time to tell her about my family.

At first, I just wanted her to get to know me. And once she did, I didn't tell her because I knew it would bring up a whole host of questions.

Like, if they're that rich, why haven't I been helicoptered back to Vegas?

Which would be a very valid question to ask.

"Kate."

She turns to me, her brow scrunched. "Kate?"

"That is your name."

"You only use it when it's about to get dangerous or we're in the middle of sex. I know we're not doing the latter..."

Shit. That sounds right. A hazard of dating such a smart woman. "I picked up a few things in town while you were grocery shopping."

I'm distracting. Again. I meant to go in the grocery store with her. Then take her shopping in the boutiques that fill the Durango downtown.

Instead, I dropped her at the grocery store, which was probably stupid and dangerous, and went to buy her gifts without her.

The thing is…

I'm starting to understand that I might want Kate in my life way longer-term than I first intended.

The more sex we have, the more I want her.

She's smart and beautiful and she looks at me with not just desire, but admiration. And not of my money.

Of me.

Like she sees a man who's worth something. But the longer I go without explaining that I'm a Kincaid…

She knows my name is Kincaid.

I technically haven't lied. Well, not until the part where I explained why we couldn't leave.

But I've kept out a fair number of details and I'm trying to figure out how and when to tell her.

"What'd you get?" she asks as she turns the stove down. "Actually. Hold that thought. I'll be right back." Then she disappears into the bathroom. I make my way out to the truck, getting out the bags I have behind the seat.

When I start to go back inside, she's coming down the porch with a bucket in hand. "Love?"

She blushes. "Toilet won't flush. I just need a bucket of water. I'll be right back."

I've got four bags in my hand, but I skip past her, setting them down on the porch. "I can get that for you."

She shakes her head, already making her way toward the river. "I'm not making you get my toilet water. I love this place, but man, it can be tough sometimes."

I'm catching up to her as she reaches the top of the bank. "Sweetheart, let me help you up and down the bank at least."

She turns to look at me as she steps, and I realize the mistake a second before it happens. She's not watching where she's going.

She steps into air, flails backwards and then disappears, sliding down the bank.

I surge forward, reaching the edge in time to watch her plunge into the water, bucket floating away.

I'm down the bank in two steps, diving in after her.

I slice through the fast-moving water, narrowly avoiding a rock and reach her in what's likely a few seconds but feels like an eternity.

Wrapping my arms around her, I push up, breaking the surface of the water with her in my arms.

She gasps in a breath, her eyes wide with fear. "Luke."

"I'm here, sweetheart." I pull her close and kiss her forehead even as she winces away. "What's wrong?"

I don't wait for the answer as I kick toward the shore, quickly reaching shallow enough ground to walk out.

My boots are slippery with all the water, but I make it up the bank anyway.

"My hip," she pushes out the words, pain making her voice high and tight.

"Fuck," I growl, heading for the house. "How bad?"

"I don't…" she sucks in another breath, "know."

I pull her closer as gently as I can. "You're going to be all right, love."

Her arms come around my neck, her face pressing into my neck. I have this irrational anger toward Mason. We should be on a helicopter back to Vegas. Kate should not…

"I'm so stupid," she's murmuring into my skin. "I've gone up and down that bank a thousand times. I just…"

"It's not your fault. I distracted you."

I bang into the house and head straight for the bedroom. Gently laying her down, I peel off her jeans, her wince cutting right through me.

As soon as I get the pants off, I can see the color already blooming on her skin.

"Shit," I rumble, pulling the pants the rest of the way down her body.

"No, it's okay," she's still breathing fast, but her voice sounds more normal. "The pain is already receding. I think it might just be a bone bruise."

My teeth grind together as I run a gentle hand up her leg. "We should see a doctor."

"Let me just do a few tests."

"On yourself?"

"With your help." She points down. "Put your hand under my knee, like this, and the other under my foot. I want to test the pain when I flex the hip."

She has me gently manipulate the hip socket, bending it this way and that. "I didn't hurt the bones." She props on her elbows to give me a smile. "That's good."

Her shirt is plastered to her body, her stomach exposed, nothing but a pair of little bikini briefs clinging to her skin.

I slowly remove my hands from her skin. "That's good. Good." And then I catch a whiff of something burning.

Standing up, I turn and head out to the kitchen. She'd turned the burner way down, but it's been sitting on simmer and the food has started to burn.

"Damn it," she yells from the bedroom. But I smile. That's my Kate.

And she is my Kate. I'm starting to see that.

Taking the food off the burner, I turn off the stove and scrape all the good food off the top into a bowl.

Kate appears in the kitchen in a fresh loose tank top. The kind with low arm holes that are adorable.

The problem?

She's not wearing a bra. I can see the curve of her tit and the tank is short enough that I've got a great view of her ass too. "What are you doing out of bed?"

"The bed is wet," she murmurs, wrinkling her nose. "And other than a nasty bruise, I think I'll be fine."

I grimace, setting down the pan. "Don't make me put you back in myself."

I know she's feeling better because she gives me a cheeky grin. "How about the couch instead?"

I set down the bowl and saunter over to where she's standing. Normally, I'd grab an ass cheek and pull her into the cradle of my hips. "You scared me."

"I'm sorry," she whispers back. "I didn't mean to frighten you, and I am so grateful you once again rescued me."

I trace the opening of one of the tank sleeves, my finger running over the side of that plump and perfect breast. "You gonna eat in just that?"

"Putting on pants seemed… difficult."

My hands skim down her belly. "You gonna be well enough to let me have you for dessert?"

Her skin instantly flushes. "I'm guessing we can manage."

"In that case, let's eat. I'm starving."

Hearing her cum will most definitely help relieve the hectic worry that's making my chest tight.

I told Kate I wasn't boyfriend material.

I meant it.

But man, she's got me acting a lot like a man who wants to be around full time. I can barely keep my hands to myself and don't even get me started on the protective bubble I want to wrap her in.

I fix two plates, bringing them out to the living room. She's stretched out on the two-seater couch, and I hand her a plate, gently lifting her legs to slide under them.

I have this feeling like this is absolutely where I'm meant to be.

CHAPTER SEVENTEEN

KATE

LUKE eats with his plate balanced on my shins and then quickly shucks the plate to the side, his hands sliding up and down my legs.

I'm trying to concentrate on my food, but when he touches me like this…

I've been a little off today because a few things haven't been quite adding up, but when I fell into that river, banging my hip on a rock, he was under me, lifting me to the surface before I was even able to register pain, let alone get myself back up.

Luke has never made me feel safer.

In a world where I've had so few people to depend on, he's starting to feel like… home. A real one.

I set my half-eaten plate to the side, not caring about food anymore, when his hands stop. "Love."

I cock my brows, looking forward to whatever he's going to say next. "Yeah?"

"You need to eat."

I blink back my surprise. This is not the sexy play I'd had in mind. "I'll finish later."

He leans closer. "Finish your dinner so I can eat you for dessert."

My lips part, and the ache between my legs flares, making me clench all the muscles to try and relieve the pressure. "How do you expect me to eat after that?"

He leans forward like he's going to touch me, but instead, he grabs my plate, and places it back in my hands. "A few more bites, kitten."

I wrinkle my nose. "You take bossy to new levels. You know that?"

"Yeah."

"You're really starting to sound like a husband or a boyfriend."

I see his jaw clench, his mouth turning down. I stuff my mouth with another bite of taco, chewing and swallowing as my face flames. Finally, I swallow it down. "Then again, what do I know? I've obviously never had a relationship. Until you, I'd never even had sex. I clearly have no experience—"

"Kate."

Crap. Using my name is a bad sign. I make to swing my legs off his lap and leave, but my hip gives a painful twinge and I whimper. His hands are instantly on me, holding me in place.

I shake my head. "Don't say my name like that. Just forget I said anything."

"I don't want to forget it," he rumbles and then his hands are sliding over my body again, from my waist, down my legs to my knees. "I agree. I am acting like a boyfriend."

My breath catches and I stare at him wide-eyed. "What?"

"Kate, whatever this is, I don't want it to end when we go back to Vegas."

"Oh," I breathe out. I wish I could sit up and kiss him. But his hands are back on my waist and he's putting just enough pressure to hold me down. "Me either."

He gives me a gorgeous smile then, one hand splaying out on my belly while the other dips between my legs. My head tips back, my lips parting as I let out a small moan. He rubs my slit with my panties still on. I try to chase the pleasure but my hip twinges again.

"Hold still, love," he whispers. "I'm going to do all the work."

"Luke," I half whine. "I don't think I can. It's too good."

He lifts his hand off my belly, sliding my underwear down my legs and then tossing them on the floor.

With my legs still mostly together, he leans down licking at my clit.

Part of me wants more, but part of me is so amped up that it's enough. His hand spreads out on my belly again, keeping me from bucking as the other nudges my uninjured leg just enough so that he can slide his finger inside me.

It's all I need, and I explode around him.

If I were a man, I think these quick orgasms would be a problem, but he only gives me a wicked grin as he gently maneuvers out from under my legs, shucking his pants down to his thighs.

For a second, I wonder what he might have in mind, but he comes around the couch, pushing the coffee table to the side and drops to his knees in front of me.

I for sure look like a cat now, one who is about to get the milk, as I give my own salacious grin at his monster cock.

"Bring it closer."

He rumbles out his satisfaction as he thrusts forward, his cock sliding between my lips.

His salty taste fills my mouth as I close my eyes and breath him in.

He tangles a hand in my hair, wrapping his fist all up in the strands. I think he's going to use the hair to move my head.

Instead, he holds me absolutely still, thrusting his hips instead.

I blow out a breath through my nose as his thrusts get harder, deeper. My eyes start to water but I don't care.

I want more of him. I want all of him.

His hand in my hair tightens, the grip so tight, it might hurt, I can't tell, my senses are so overwhelmed.

He's spitting and growling, his body taut, and I know he's going to break.

I relax, greedy for more of him and when he starts to cum, I swallow him down, my eyes closing as I drink him in.

His hand loosens first, smoothing the strands. "Shit. Kate. Did I hurt—"

I look up at him, wondering just how glassy my eyes look. "No. I mean, a little. But I liked it."

He bends down, kissing me with a ferocity that steals my breath as our tongues tangle.

He lifts up, just a few inches looking down at me, his breathing still heavy.

"Luke."

"Yeah, love?"

"I think…" I swallow down a lump. "I think I might be falling…" I can't finish. Afraid the words will break us into a million pieces.

But he cups my face in one hand the other cradling my skull. "What happens when the summer's over? When you're done working for Doctor Douchebag?"

Luke and his nicknames…

I shrug. "I go back to New York. I've got two more years of med school."

"New York," he looks thoughtfully into the space over the couch. "I could be down with that."

My brows lift. Is he talking about going back to the East Coast with me? Holy shit.

I push up on one elbow. "Are you serious?"

"Only if it's cool with you. I'm not trying—" I cut him off by kissing him again. My arms are around his neck, my tongue in his mouth.

He lets me devour him as he pulls me up, lifting me in his arms. I finally pull back. "Where are we going?"

"Bed."

"But… I got the sheets all wet."

"We'll have to share the dry side," he gives me a wicked grin. "Looks like you're sleeping on top of me."

"You're really going to come back to New York with me? What about your job? Aren't your employers missing you?"

A shadow crosses his face. “It’s a family job. And I’ll get another. I’m kind of shit at it anyway.”

“Shit at construction?”

He doesn’t say anything as he settles me on his chest, wrapping his arms around me.

I sigh out my pleasure.

I’ve got the most gorgeous man underneath me who is everything I never dreamed I could have. Cool, bad-ass, sweet, straightforward.

He’s everything I never thought I could have.

I wrap my arms tighter around him, nuzzling my face into the crook of his neck.

“Do I get to meet your family before I go?”

“Arabella and Roman, absolutely. Leo too. Mason, though…” His arms tighten around me. “He’s as tough as they come. Only Charlotte can tame him, and sometimes not even she softens his sharp edges.”

“Mason Kincaid?” The name rings with a familiarity, but I’m tired. Satiated. And I find myself drifting off to sleep before I can put all the thoughts together.

CHAPTER EIGHTEEN

KATE

I WAKE to the smell of fresh coffee and bacon.

Sitting up, my hip twinges but it's a manageable pain. I stretch, and then get up. There is no laundry here, and I'm running out of underwear and shirts. There is no washer. There is an old-style ringer in the shed at the back of the property or we're heading to a laundromat.

I should have picked some up while we were in Durango.

Instead, I grab one of Luke's T-shirts and slide it over my head, pushing my arms through the sleeves.

It falls to my mid-thighs and stretching again, I walk out of the bedroom, into the tiny hall and into the bathroom.

"Hold up," Luke calls from the kitchen. He appears, just as I'm sticking a toothbrush into my mouth.

He stands in the doorway, not saying a word until I spit out the toothpaste and rinse my mouth. "Everything all right?" I ask, pulling my sleep-tousled hair over one shoulder.

"Dandy," he answers, leaning against the jam. "You look amazing this morning."

I lift my brows with a laugh. "In your giant shirt?"

"In my shirt. Yeah." And then he reaches for me, pulling me into his arms and kissing my mouth. It's playful and intimate as his hand creeps up into my hair, cradling my head.

"It smells like you," I whisper against his lips as I wind my arms around his neck.

His other hand skims up the back of my thigh. "And now it's going to smell like you. When you change, I want it back."

Holy crap, he knows how to get me going. I lean back, my heart beginning to skip in my chest.

He kisses me again and then lets me go, pushing off the jam. "Don't want to burn your bacon."

"My bacon?"

"Yeah. I'd eat the burnt stuff, but you might not want yours as cooked as mine."

I close the bathroom door and finish up, then head to the kitchen. Luke has started eggs.

I take a seat at a kitchen chair, and he hands me a cup of black coffee. Smiling, I take a sip.

"I'll call Mason today, see if we can head back to Vegas."

"If we don't," I take another sip, "I need to do some laundry." Now that the call with Dr. Shrewsbury is done, I'm in way less of a hurry to get back. I've even wondered if I want to do the internship.

Do I want to be a surgeon? If I didn't care what anyone thought of me, what would I do with my life?

I've been so focused on being as successful as possible, I haven't stopped to ask questions like, what brings me joy? What do I love?

I think back to the kids we rescued on the side of the road. I liked helping them. Liked their adorable smiles and their sweet voices.

Maybe that's where my future lies. Either way, there have been some blessings in what's happened the past few days. One of them was meeting Luke, but the other is just taking a moment, away from the noise of life, to really think about me and what I want.

"Laundry?" he asks, quirking a brow.

"Yeah. I'm out of shirts," I point to his.

"We can definitely take care of that." He leans down and kisses me again, despite the coffee breath and then returns to the stove to flip the eggs. "And as much as I like having you in my shirt, when we go out, I've got a few more things you can wear."

A minute later, he sets down a heaping plate in front of me. I wrinkle my nose. "How much do you think I eat?"

"I know you didn't finish your tacos last night," he responds, setting his own plate down, which has the same amount of food as mine.

I am not a male who needs to eat a mountain of food, and as he disappears from the room, I take some of the food from my plate and dump it on his.

He comes back, and narrows his eyes at first my plate, and then his. But he doesn't say a word as he sets down several bags at my feet.

My food forgotten, I cock my head. "What's all this?"

"Stuff I picked up for you in town."

I open the first bag and pull out a Dyson hair dryer. My mouth drops open. "What is this?"

"The hair dryer in this place stinks and I know you like to dry your hair."

"But..." I stare at the thing. I could never afford one. "These are like six hundred dollars."

He shrugs.

How much money did Mason send him?

In the next bag are more underwear. But these are not from Walmart. It's lace and cut to flatter, the fabric slipping through my fingers.

In the next bag are designer shirts. The kind that would look amazing on me, but I don't ever buy because... "How much did all this cost?"

"Don't worry," he says, taking a big bite of eggs. "I got you."

But that thing that's been nagging is back and it's biting right at the surface. "How did you get Doctor Shrewsbury to change his mind?"

Luke grimaces. "I told you."

"No. Not really. And how..." But then, it hits me. I saw this billboard by the airport. A massive tunnel in the heart of Las Vegas was being advertised. And it was by Kincaid Enterprises.

I gasp, dropping the shirt, the garment slipping to the floor. "Construction?"

"Kate," he says, reaching out a hand. "I am in construction."

"Your family is building the largest construction project that Vegas has ever seen. It will bring in billions."

He shrugs. "Actually, I'm building it."

The blood rushes from my head, dizziness taking over. He didn't *not* tell me. He said he was a Kincaid. That he was in construction, that he was the rival of Vincent and Vigo. But this is huge...

"But? Why? You should have told me. About all of this. You're like... like... rich."

He winces. "I kind of assumed you knew. I can't meet anyone in Vegas who doesn't either recognize me or my name. It was nice for you to just think of me as a regular guy. To like me for just me."

That really makes sense. I get that. "But why didn't you tell me yesterday? When I was freaking out about my internship why didn't you just say 'everyone in the world does what I ask them?'"

His grimace tells me that he's got a reason and I'm not going to like it. But my brain is spinning now.

"Why hasn't your family just sent a whole security detail to collect us?"

The grimace turns into a wince. "Kate." He scrubs his hands down his face. "Try to understand."

"I don't. Explain it."

"I messed up the permits." He shakes his head. "Me and my stupid brain."

My heart stutters in my chest.

"It's why I was there that night. I was trying to fix my mistake. A billion dollar company about to be flushed down the toilet because I transposed a couple of dates..." I can see the anguish on his face. "It was my mistake to correct."

I lean forward, hurting for him. But also looking for answers.

"Mason only ever brought me into the business because I was family. Because my mom raised Roman and Arabella."

His face is twisted in pain. "Luke, you're the strongest man I know."

He shakes his head. "I'm worth more to my family dead than I am alive."

Confusion makes me pull back. "What does that mean?"

His face goes slack, the color draining. "I… uh…"

"What does it mean, Luke?" My voice is loud and tight, as my hands come to the table.

"It means that blood, my blood, was found in the Vendettis' car and…"

But suddenly it's clear. "Do people think they killed you? Are Vincent and Vigo on the run? Is Mason afraid they're joining Gorilla to come after us?" Fear stiffens all my muscles.

"They're in jail."

I blink several times, trying to clear away my confusion. "But if they're in jail, why haven't we gone back?" But even as I ask, I know. They're in jail for murder. Luke can't go back.

He's here playing house with me, interrupting my entire life, because it's convenient for him.

Bile rises from my stomach, up my esophagus, as my hand covers my mouth.

Did he even mean his offer to go to New York with me? I gasp in a breath, trying to clear my spinning head, as I push up from the table.

He stands too, reaching for me, but I jerk away from him, spinning and stomping into the living room.

I'm only in a T-shirt. I'm not even wearing underwear, but I grab the truck keys and the phone, sprinting out the door and down the steps.

My feet are bare, and tears are blurring my eyes, but I hear the squeak of the screen door as Luke comes out on the porch too. "Kate. Wait."

"I can't believe this," I gasp, as I reach the truck and wrench open the door. "I missed my internship start date for your family's business."

I point an angry finger at him. "I helped you that night."

He slowly walks down the porch. "I helped you too, love."

"Don't call me that."

"I'll always help you."

"Except when you're totally fucking up my life."

My God. I am my mother after all. I found a man who selfishly blew up my entire life. I push up into the cab of the truck, jamming the key into the ignition.

"Kate. Sweetheart. You can't go. You're not even dressed."

I can feel the tears welling in my eyes. Not because this is new or unexpected, but because this is old. I've done this before. Granted, I was next to my mother as she tossed our shit into the back of some crap car, screaming at some man before we sped away.

Jesus. I press the brake and turn the key, knowing Luke is right. How can I roll up anywhere like this?

But it's a moot point because nothing happens.

The truck doesn't turn over. It's dead.

CHAPTER NINETEEN

Luke

I walk up to the open window, leaning against the frame of the door.

Kate has her face against the steering wheel, crying.

I want to touch her so badly, it hurts. "Babe."

"Don't call me that."

She lifts her face, tears staining her cheeks. "Please, sweetheart."

"Don't call me that either." She reaches for the handle of the truck, and I back up so she can get out.

"What do I call you then?"

She snorts. "Kate is fine. Katherine better. All those nicknames were part of faking me out, weren't they?"

"Faking you out?" I've got a bad feeling about this.

"Even before I realized you were rich, I should have known a guy like you wouldn't ever want me."

I cross my arms. "Why wouldn't I want you?"

She gestures down her front. "We've been over this. I don't look like the girl who gets a guy like you. Brown hair. Skinny hips. Deadbeat mom." She waves her hands and my T-shirt rides up, giving me the tiniest peek between her legs.

Maybe I should carry her into the house and make her cum until she forgets this whole thing. Tempting…

"That's bullshit. You're the hottest woman I've ever met."

She shakes her head.

"And my dad was definitely as bad as your mom. I get it."

Her shoulders go limp as she turns, starting down the driveway. "Where are you going?"

"I'm leaving," she fires back.

I've got her by the waist in a second, hauling her up over my shoulder.

"Put me down," she hits my back with her small fist. I barely feel it.

But when I smack my hand across her bare ass, she jumps like it stings. "Do you want your spanking first or would you rather that I eat you out until you scream?"

"What?" she gasps, her hands splaying out on my back.

"Look…" I'd like to set her down, but she's not leaving in nothing but a T-shirt. "I get parents who are a mess. But I had one bad one and one good one. And my mom taught me that when you care about someone, you work shit out and apologize when you're wrong."

"I'm pretty sure that means you're getting the spanking," she huffs.

That makes me grin. "We both know I'm the alpha in the bedroom, baby." And I smack her ass again. "But for you, I'll take a beating if you need to give me one."

I feel her wilt against me. "Is that your way of saying sorry?"

I'm up on the porch, and back in the house before I set her down, but I keep a good hold on her. "I'm sorry I didn't tell you the whole truth. And I'm sorry that you're stuck here playing dead with me. And I'm sorry that I didn't tell you about my family."

"They're sacrificing my future for theirs."

"I made Doctor Shrewsbury…"

She shakes her head. "He's never going to give me a good rec or help me get the next coveted spot. I may as well not go."

Fuck. She's not wrong. That's how big dicks work. "Kate."

Her shoulders curl in. "Was it all a lie? What we said last night?"

I pull her into my arms, burying my face in her hair. I can tell her the truth. None of it was a lie, but I also know she's not going to believe me. "No. And all I ask is that you stick around long enough for me to prove it."

She shakes her head against my chest. "It's not the same now."

"Well, I will tell you what is the same, Gorilla is still on our tail. And I don't want you meeting him alone."

That makes her stiffen and she leans back, her eyes wide as they meet mine. Had she forgotten about the giant ape following us?

"Besides," I curl a palm around her naked ass. "You can't go walking down the road in your bare feet and no pants."

Her cheeks flush with color. "I know that."

I plant a kiss on the top her head and then her temple, the bend of her jaw, down her neck. "I know I fucked up. I did warn you I'm not the brightest."

"Don't give me that bullshit," she scoffs. "I know how good you are at a ton of shit."

I smile into her neck. "But I nearly cost my family everything. I was trying to make it right."

She draws in a deep breath, pushing those fantastic tits against my chest. "I know."

"But give me a chance to make it right with you too."

She shakes her head. "I don't see how. I know you lied to me about why we stayed, and I know you lied about New York."

That makes me lift my head. "I did not lie about New York."

"You're not leaving your family to be a poor student with me."

"Who said anything about being poor? I would like to start a garage. Maybe work on old cars. I'm shit at real estate anyway. You would not believe how much paperwork there is. Makes my head hurt."

Kate's mouth drops open. "You're serious?"

"Very."

I slide my hand over her ass, splaying my fingers over the small of her back under the T-shirt. "Now how about that spanking? Just for fun? The idea of your ass all red..."

She pushes out of my arms, glaring at me. "I don't think so."

Shit. She's still upset. "You need more space. I get it." Then I cock my head to the side. "I could just eat you out, baby. You can leave me with a giant boner as my punishment."

"Warmer, but no," she says as she heads for the bathroom and grabs a towel. "I'm washing up. Think you can fix the truck? I really do need to do laundry."

"You got it, love."

I see her mouth pinch at the nickname, but at least she's not telling me to fuck off. I'm going to have to figure out how to make things right with Kate.

Because honestly, I can't imagine my life without her at this point.

She stops in front of me, with her towel in hand. "I wouldn't have really left."

"I'm glad to hear it." I want to pull her close again, but this time, I drop down on my knees, pressing my face to her belly, as I hold her bare thighs in my hands. "I would have been crazy with worry."

"I don't date, Luke. I mean, obviously. You know that better than anyone. But the reason is, I've always worried that I couldn't trust myself. And now I'm worried that you just proved my worst fears about myself true..."

Fuck me. "That's what happened with me and the tunnel. Everything I hated about myself bit me right in the ass. Roman got hurt, tunnel project gone, enemies got me on the run."

Her hands come to my shoulders. "I get that. But how long is it going to take you to trust yourself again?"

Is she saying she won't be able to trust me? Or herself around me?

My teeth clench together as my jaw goes granite hard. Here I am, fucking it up again.

But I push up, her body folding over my shoulder once again. "What are you doing?"

"Carrying you down the bank," I grunt. "If we ever come back to this cabin, I'm building stairs."

"You can do that? Build stairs?"

I'm back out the door and heading toward the stream. "Can't do the math, but I get by. It's when I start thinking about shit, I mess it up." And that is the truest thing I've ever said.

She wiggles on my shoulder, her ass pushing up into my hand. I hold her a little tighter, my fingers digging into her ass cheek, not wanting her to fall.

"We've both got our shit, don't we?"

"Truth."

"What would you do if you didn't really think about it? Right now?"

I trot down the bank, skipping over a few rocks. "Fuck you until you forget everything but the feel of my cock."

"Okay."

I stop at the bottom, on the edge of the water. "Okay?"

"I have no idea how to fight with a guy. My mom is my only example, and the move I just pulled, getting in the truck, was all hers. So, let's try it your way. What have I got to lose?"

CHAPTER TWENTY

KATE

I HAVE EVERYTHING TO LOSE.

My dignity.

My self-worth.

My belief that I can break the pattern of my mother's behavior. Maybe I picked the wrong guy, which means I'm doomed anyway.

Or maybe I've found my Mark and it's on me to not blow it up. Not let Luke go the way my mom let the one man go who was ever going to love us.

I don't think about it anymore as Luke holds me with one arm, yanking his old jeans down his thighs.

He's right, we really do have a problem with clothes. We can't seem to wait long enough to get them off.

Because his jeans only make it far enough down his legs to let his cock out, and then he's lifting me up and plunging me down on the length of him.

It feels so good, I'm so full that I lean out, arching so that he's even deeper inside me.

And then his hand smacks my ass. Hard.

My eyes fly open.

"That is for trying to run away."

He's deep in me and we're not moving. My legs start to tremble, wanting to squeeze his waist and lift myself up to feel the friction. "And what's your punishment for lying?"

His teeth grit. "I don't get to cum."

Oh. That does seem appropriate.

He lifts me up and plunges me back down, smacking my ass again. But this time the pain only heightens the pleasure, and I cry out, the kind of noise that can't be mistaken.

It feels amazing and I want more.

"Christ, Kate, you fucking kill me," he grunts as he lifts me again, plunging me back down on his shaft as he smacks my ass again.

"Why?" It comes out like keening moan, my ass on fire, my body humming with the pleasure.

"You're so fucking perfect. I want to cum so bad."

Is he suffering? Good. But I lose my focus as he keeps hammering me. The sweet torture of pain and pleasure build to heights that are better than any time before this. I gasp for air as he keeps pushing me harder and faster until I finally break apart, shattering around him, my screams echoing around us.

He falls to his knees, landing in the water, his face full of torture.

He's still inside me, his arms around me as his forehead falls to mine. "Promise me you won't try to leave like that again?"

"I promise. Now you promise me, no more lies. No more deception."

"Promise," he grinds out between his teeth. The tension around his eyes tells me that he's trying so hard to behave. To keep his promise of not cumming.

But this wasn't supposed to be easy.

And to drive my point home, I flex my hips.

His eyes squeeze shut, his arms squeezing me tighter. "Kate."

"I'm taking you right to the edge," I whisper. "You're going to beg."

His eyes snap open. I've been happy to do as he's asked me in the bedroom. It always means my pleasure.

But he likes to dominate, and this is his punishment. I took mine.

"Oh, baby girl," he rumbles, his eyes filling with fire. "I'll fucking beg you right now. Never try to leave like that again."

"That's not begging." And I squeeze him with my legs, lifting up his cock only to slide back down, pulling him into my body again.

Keeping hold of him with my legs, I peel his shirt off my body. Then I wrap my arms around his neck, thrusting my breasts up.

He drops his face into them, sucking one of my nipples into his mouth. I grab a fistful of his hair and pull, lifting his face to mine. And then I kiss him like I've never kissed before. It's tongue and teeth, pain and pleasure, as I slide up him and sink back down again.

His hands are on my hips now, helping to push me up, pull me down. His mouth is hot on mine, his chest rumbling with the need that's building inside him.

I take one of my heels and dig into his ass. Hard. Every part of my body invites him deeper, harder.

He's spitting words I can't even understand as I dig my fingernails into the skin of his neck.

Another orgasm is building inside me too. I try to fight it, knowing that I could lose myself and forfeit his punishment if I do.

His fingers dig into my hips, his grip so tight, I think he might leave marks.

I don't care.

My body is chasing pleasure again, even though I know I need to stay focused. His cock swells inside me and I know he's close.

I pull his hair harder, wrenching his head back as I look into his eyes. "Tell me the truth."

I don't ride him less. No. It's harder.

"The truth?"

"Do you want me? Not just for today, but for tomorrow and the next day, and the day after that?"

His teeth are clenched, the corded muscles of his neck so taut, they look like they might break.

"Fucking hell, love. I want you forever."

I forget to hold back, another orgasm rips through me. He snarls, his hands so tight on my hips as the snarl turns into these broken grunts and growls.

"Forever?" I manage to gasp out. "Like forever, forever?"

"I fucking love you, Kate." And he slams into me again. "Like die-for-you kind of love."

I lift up, despite my muscles feeling like jelly and slam down on him again. I know what I'm doing.

This was supposed to be his punishment. But I'm going to have find another way. Because I want him filling me.

He erupts inside me, feral as he finishes.

I wilt into him, so spent, I think I might have to go back to sleep for another eight hours. "Holy shit."

He kisses my shoulder, then up my neck. "Do you love me too?"

Did I not say it? I can't hold back as I breathe in the air he's pushed out. "Yes. I love you."

He kisses me again, as he sits down, my legs are still around him. "So, it's me and you."

I lift my face and look into his eyes. "How does your family fit into that?"

I see the grimace and I know that his family is still a problem. There is what's good for me. And then there is what's good for them.

I love this man. But am I giving up my future so that he can play dead to help his family close the next major deal?

I slowly push up, splashing in the shallow water, before I sink deeper, letting the cool water wash away the heat of my skin.

It's not completely fair. I don't have anyone that I have to factor in. Mark is there for me, but we don't even spend most holidays together.

I've never had people I'm loyal to like that.

But I don't know that I'm giving up my whole career for the interests of people I've never even met.

So maybe Luke isn't a bum. Maybe he really loves me. But I'm not sure it's enough.

Luke shucks off his soaked pants and joins me in the water. "What are you thinking?"

I plant my feet on the bottom, the water coming up to just over my boobs. "I don't know. I guess that I have to go back soon. I heard everything you said about Gorilla. But if I don't go back to Vegas, I should return to New York. This summer is critical and—"

He grimaces. "You can't spend it hiding out in this cabin."

I nod.

He runs a hand through his wet hair. "I think I might have a solution. But first, I need to fix the truck."

Hope rises in my chest. "Really?" My arms are around him, my lips pressing to his.

He kisses me back as he pulls me close. "While I do that, why don't you think of my real punishment? Because that last one backfired into the best orgasm of my entire life."

I give a breathless laugh. "Me too."

And to be honest, the spanking wasn't really a punishment either. It turned out amazing.

Since we're in the water, I wash up and then head back to the cottage. I dress, marveling at the new clothes.

Luke dresses too. "I'm going to go work on the truck."

Is that his plan? Are we leaving? I nod. "I'll clean up breakfast and then maybe you can tell me about this plan?"

He winks. "You got it, gorgeous."

I feel my skin heat as he heads out the door.

CHAPTER TWENTY-ONE

Luke

I skip down the steps, whistling to myself.

Lifting the hood of the truck, I take a cursory look. "What's wrong, Alice?" I ask the truck. "Were you just trying to keep Kate from making a big mistake?"

She scared the shit out of me when she got in that truck. Funny thing was, I slowed down instead of sped up.

Kate likes my dominance in the bedroom. But when it comes to her heart, I sense it: she's fragile. Afraid.

She likes my relaxed and confident energy. She bathes in it like the way we wash in the river.

If I'd chased her too hard, I'd have lost her.

As it was, we ended up in the river, doing the kind of dirty things I've only dreamed about.

I'm a man with experience. And money. But the thing about Kate, what's always been different, is that she wants me as much as I want her. She doesn't just submit, she fucking loves it.

She's smart and beautiful, incredibly sweet, and so fucking vulnerable. Mason sent me ten grand. It's more than enough for me to get across the country. Hell, we could trade in Alice and buy an RV with that money. Camp.

I could have her back to New York in a week. Press her professor to lie and tell her advisor that he's the reason the position fell through.

This gives Kate what she needs and still allows Mason the room to maneuver into a better position.

No one will recognize me there and my family can finish the deal. I have to ask Kate. But first, I need Alice to run.

I pull out the spark plug, blowing on it as I inspect the terminal. Might be the battery. Alice didn't turn over at all.

But I'm fixated enough, leaning down deep into the engine that I don't realize I'm not alone until I hear a twig snap just to my right.

And before I can lift up, the hood comes slamming down on my head, pinning me under the heavy metal.

My arms are under my body and when I try to push up, the hood doesn't budge.

"Fuck."

"Sex make you soft," a deep voice with a thick Italian accent rumbles as Gorilla's face appears between the narrow gap between the hood and the truck.

A lead ball settles in my stomach as I try again to push the hood up. But Gorilla has got it firmly in place.

It only takes a second for me to understand that Gorilla heard or saw what Kate and I did down by the water.

Rage rumbles through me. Kate is for me alone. No one else. But I bottle it, knowing I've only got one chance. "How are Vigo and Vincent enjoying prison?"

"They out soon," he spits back. "And you pay."

There is someone who is going to pay. "For?"

"Stealing," Gorilla points toward the house, grinning like a fool.

If he thinks Kate belongs to Vincent, he's going to know what my wrath feels like. "Mine," I spit back.

"I want keep her too," Gorilla leers at me. "She make pretty noise."

Fucker. He was spying like a bitch. "Stay away from her."

"No. You." He eases up the pressure for a split second and I use it to get my arm out from under me, pushing up and lashing out to grab him.

But I'm too slow. Or this was his plan all along. Because the hood slams down on my head and the world goes black…

CHAPTER TWENTY-TWO

KATE

THE SOUND of a loud metal bang makes me lift my head.

Dropping the sponge, I head to the living room. The view out the window makes my blood run cold.

It's Gorilla and he's got Luke trapped.

Spinning, I race to the bedroom and throw open the closet door. I know Mark keeps a shotgun in here.

Sure enough, it's there. Next to it is a box of cartridges.

I haven't fired this gun, or any gun, in years, but I remember the basics as I release the lever and break open the barrel, stuffing two shells in before I close it up. Starting down the hall, I switch off the safety.

That's when I hear the hood of the truck slam again. My hands shaking, I push open the screen door just in time to see Gorilla come around the truck.

My heart nearly stops when I see Luke on the ground.

Gorilla sees me too and stops. "Ciao, bellissima."

I don't respond as I lift the shotgun and wrap my finger around the trigger. I don't think, I just pull.

Gorilla dives behind the truck but I see his body jerk and I think I hit him somewhere. But I don't drop the gun.

I've got another shot.

And I doubt this is over.

I'm shaking as I scan the yard. I don't want to leave the porch. I'm covered on at least one side with the house behind me. If I leave its safety, I give him a chance to get behind me.

Then again, I haven't seen a single movement since the first shot.

Is he dead behind the truck? Did I just kill a man?

A little sob catches in my throat.

I'm a doctor. Almost. I save lives...

But that's when I see him. Crouched low, he's almost reached the woods toward the road.

I gasp in a breath again as I aim the gun. But before I can squeeze off another shot, he's gone. Disappearing into the woods.

I race down the stairs to Luke. Setting down the gun, I'm relieved when I touch him and he's still warm.

Taking a deep breath, I check for a pulse, it's there and strong. I don't see any visible injuries, but I quickly run my hands over him, checking for contusions or broken bones, but it's just a quick scan.

Grabbing the gun, I get up. I hold it out as I slowly spin, making sure Gorilla hasn't doubled back.

I don't see him, but I do see the trail of blood. I choke as I race back up the steps and into the house, grabbing the phone.

I'm back outside in a second, sliding to the ground next to Luke, the gun still in my hand.

I need help.

Picking up, I call the last number on the call list.

A deep male voice picks up on the second ring. "Luke?"

"No," I gasp. "Please. It's Kate."

"Kate," he repeats. "What's wrong?"

"Mason?"

"It's me."

"Luke is hurt. We need help."

"Hurt? How?"

"Gorilla... I mean Guerriero is here. I don't know how he knocked Luke out. I was in the house."

"He knocked Luke out? Where is Guerriero now?"

"I'm not sure," I cry, a sob escaping my lips. I can feel myself getting hysterical. I try to breathe. "I shot him and he ran off."

"You shot him?" Mason's voice rises with every word.

"I know. It's bad." Luke moans and I lower the gun, reaching for him, placing my hand over his chest.

"You're fine," Mason says, his voice taking on this soothing tone. "You did the right thing. What's wrong with Luke?"

"Knocked out," I say, my voice breaking. "I don't know how."

He holds the phone away from his mouth, barking several orders, but he must cover the mouthpiece because I can't hear the words, just the tone.

"You still have the gun?"

"Yeah."

"Bullets?"

"One in the barrel, more in the house."

"What did you shoot him with?"

"Bird shot, I think."

"You probably didn't kill him then," Mason says. "And I'm sending help. The chopper will be there in half an hour."

"Chopper? Half hour?"

"This is important, Kate. Keep the gun up. Keep alert."

I draw in a shaky breath. "Keep alert."

Luke's heartbeat is strong under my hand has he moans again. I lift his head the slightest bit, feeling his skull.

He's got a lump on the back of his head. I can only hope that's the worst of his injuries. "Luke?"

I hear Mason rumble as Luke's eyes blink open. "Luke," I gasp out, relief making me limp. "There you are."

His stare back at me is blank, which has me stiffening in fear again.

"Here I am?" It's a question as he slowly lifts a hand, looking at me in confusion. "What did you say my name was again?"

"Fuck," Mason whispers as I give Luke a tremulous smile.

"Your name is Luke Kincaid. We're at my stepfather's cabin."

"And who are you, gorgeous?"

Well, at least he's using nicknames, even if it's not the right one. "My name is Kate." Medical experience is kicking in. "But your preferred nickname for me is love."

"Love," he inspects my face and then smiles. "I've got good taste."

I feel myself blush all over again. Does he really think so? Granted, this meet and greet isn't much less dramatic then our real first meeting. But I needed rescuing then and I was worried that was part of my appeal. "You also like kitten, princess, and beautiful. Nicknames are kind of your thing."

He reaches up and strokes my cheek. "Are old trucks my thing too?"

"Kate," Mason rumbles in my ear. "Don't forget to keep watch."

My eyes snap up and with it, the barrel of the gun.

"We have trouble?" Luke asks, his voice taking on a serious tone. I look back down at him for the briefest second. Is he working himself up to protect me? Oh, this man.

"Put Luke on the phone," Mason says.

"It's your cousin and business associate, Mason Kincaid," I say and place the phone against Luke's ear.

I scan the woods, doing as Mason said, but I can still hear the conversation.

"Hello?"

"Luke. Are you all right?"

"No idea."

"Then you're fine. If you can do one thing, it's truck through a pile of shit and then you just keep going."

"Got it."

"I've sent help, the helicopter will be there in the next fifteen minutes."

"Helicopter?" Luke looks down at his grease-covered shirt, pulling it away from his chest. "I'm at an old cabin with an even older truck. This doesn't seem like a helicopter setting, and I don't seem like a helicopter guy."

Mason pauses. "It's a really long story. I think Kate can tell you most of it. But to fill in the details for you, you're sleeping with her, but it's a… convenient arrangement."

My heart stutters in my chest. It's my fear said out loud. Did Luke tell Mason this? Is that how he really feels? Is he still lying to me? Manipulating?

My fingers flex on his chest and Luke's eyes meet mine. There is no wince, his gaze is as steady as a mountain. Then again, he has no memory. "I see."

"What matters is getting our business to the next level to provide the safety and security we need to survive." Mason clears his throat. "It's where you are invaluable."

"I understand." Luke's eyes still hold mine.

"And she's got medical training, so listen to her about any injuries."

Sleeping with her. The words echo through my head again as I rest Luke's head in my lap.

It's the dismissive tone. Like he expected nothing less, and I mean very little.

Then again… will Luke remember any of the promises we made? Did he mean them?

My breath hitches as the distant sound of chopper blades punctuate the quiet. I'm not getting an answer now. About a million questions will come before this one.

But in my head, the words echo. Do we have a future? My heart wants the answer to be yes.

But I've always worried that I'm a convenient distraction before Luke goes back to his family and his life.

And Mason just validated my worst fear.

CHAPTER TWENTY-THREE

LUKE

THE CHOPPER TRIP to a small city is followed by a plane ride to I don't know where. It's a mystery. Through it all, Kate's hand is laced with mine.

I heard what Mason said about sleeping with this woman.

He hinted that I was using her. That she was part of this plan to elevate our business, nothing more.

Waking without memory is the oddest sensation. I searched but nothing was there. Then, as I looked at her face, though I couldn't remember, I could still feel.

This woman has my heart. If I doubted, her touch said it all. She ran her hands over me like I was the most valuable thing in the world.

And her story about my nicknames…

She likes them. And if I call her *love*… Then I love her. Why do I know that about myself?

The moment I heard Mason's voice, a ton of shit came back. My mom. My childhood. Roman. Arabella.

Odd. I can't picture Mason yet. His voice sparked my memory, but his words were so cold. Am I that man? Cold? Calculating?

And I can't remember a fucking thing about where I live, what I do for work. How I ended up in the woods in a cabin.

My head is pounding.

But I bring Kate's hand, still laced with mine, to my lips and kiss the back of it, feeling the silk of her skin against my lips.

It's a funny thing. I feel like the really important shit is floating to the surface in a way that's providing so much clarity.

Kate told me about the tunnel project I apparently care about. About my worries I'd failed my family.

The way I struggle with numbers and even paperwork.

She told me about Gorilla, another one of my nicknames.

I listened to the whole thing, not saying much. Kate puts her head on my shoulder, the small plane humming above the clouds. "So all of Las Vegas thinks I'm dead?"

"Yeah."

"And I just went along with it?"

"I guess. I don't really know that part."

"And I went to a sight in the middle of the night to close a deal?"

"Yes. And got shot. Nearly. That part I know, and I was even there for most of it."

I shake my head. "Well, I guess I know my role in this company."

"What?"

"I'm the guy who does the shit jobs. The one they put on the dangerous stuff. And I just power through, apparently."

But I also heard what Kate told me about my own insecurities. Do I power through because I feel inferior?

Does Mason take advantage of that?

Her fingers slide over my arm. "I can't say for certain. We haven't talked about your family much."

"Why not?"

She hesitates. "You didn't want to tell me at first. You wanted me to just get to know you. But then…"

"But Mason…" I fill in, looking down at her. I can tell by her wince that I'm on the right track. "What did he do? Or ask me to do?"

She shakes her head. "This is a conversation for when you have all your memories."

"I want to have it now."

She bites at her lip. She's beautiful and adorable and the feel of her hands are like magic.

"How serious are we?" I try again.

"We've only known each other a short time."

"But we're getting serious quickly, aren't we?"

"Yeah," I see relief shine in her eyes as her shoulders wilt. "I think so. I mean you said so, but…"

I'm getting it. "Is this different from your other relationships?"

Her eyes go wide and then she winces. "I haven't had other boyfriends. You're my first," she whispers. "But we honestly haven't put any labels on what we're doing yet."

I lean forward and kiss her forehead. I haven't kissed her yet because… I don't remember doing it before and I wasn't sure if I was welcome or not. I have no idea where we are on the intimacy scale.

But the taste of her skin, a hint of citrus, a bit of sweet, a salty musk that's all her own. I could lick her like a popsicle.

"What labels would you put on our relationship?"

"Luke. It's not fair of me to lead you in any direction."

"Mason did not have those qualms."

"I heard," she frowns.

"Tell me the truth."

"We told each other that we loved each other," she looks at her lap.

"So why does Mason think that you're not important to me?"

"Because," she lets out a long slow breath. "Everyone in Vegas thinks you're dead. And the guys who the police think killed you are the same ones trying to steal your project."

My brow furrows. "But…"

"If you stayed at the cabin, hidden, then they keep those men in prison while permits go through."

"And you agreed to stay with me?"

"I…" She draws in a breath. "You lied to me. Told me they were still a threat."

I sit back in my seat, my back thumping the cushioned chair. That's a shit thing to do to a woman I said I loved. "Anything else?"

"I…" She lets go of my hand for the first time all day, rubbing her palms on her own thighs. "I missed the start of my internship."

"Fuck," I scrub my hands down my face. "And Mason asked me to do this?"

"Yes. I think so."

The picture is getting very sharp.

It's funny how when you take your assumptions out, how clear situations become.

"Do you know when I'll get all these memories back?" I turn to look her, wishing I could say to her that I'd never hurt her.

She shakes her head. "It's different for every person. The fact that you already have them returning would indicate that this is very short term, and you'll remember everything soon."

I look into her eyes and this memory punches me in the gut. Fucking her in a river. It doesn't sound like the most romantic moment except…

I can see her face as she cums, feel her pussy around my cock as I explode. And then she looks into my eyes.

It's like falling in love all over again.

More memories trickle in. Her insecurity over a waitress. The way she held some kid in my truck.

I have no idea why we'd have kids in my truck.

It doesn't matter.

"Kate," my voice is rough with emotion. I flick her buckle open and then grab her by her hips, tugging her into my lap.

I hear the small sound of relief that leaves her lips. Has she wanted to be in my arms?

I settle her against my chest, pushing her head into the crook of my neck. "The next time we're on a plane, we'll join the mile high club," I rumble.

She gives the smallest laugh into the chords of my neck, as she burrows deeper.

"But I swear, sweetheart, from now on, it's me and you."

She shakes her head against my neck. "Don't promise anything. Not yet."

"Why not?"

She tips her head back, looking into my eyes. "Because. First you need to remember. Then we can talk."

The plane shifts, banking to one side.

I look down to see the Rockies to my left. I don't know how, but I recognize Aspen. "Where'd we fly out of?"

"Durango," Kate says. "The cabin's near there."

The plane lands fifteen minutes later, and several security types meet us with black suits and earpieces.

If I didn't know that Mason was my family, I'd swear that I was in trouble here.

We're shuffled into the back of a limo, Kate looking around the interior like she's been transported to another universe.

"Funny," she nibbles at her lip. "You don't fit here like you do with Alice."

"Alice?" Is she talking about another woman. There is no way…

"The truck. That's what you named her."

Alice. I like it. Chuckling, I slouch back in the seat and open the mini fridge to my left, finding a bottle of champagne inside.

I've still got a splitting headache, but Kate should have a drink. It's been a day.

I pop the cork, pouring her a glass.

She watches me, her head cocked. "Well. You know how to pour champagne."

I wink. "I've got class, baby."

She takes the glass and takes a sip, hiding a smile. "You're starting to sound like yourself."

Am I? That's good, I guess. I mean, I want to know myself, remember.

But in some ways, I feel like I've remembered enough. Roman and Arabella. My mother. Kate.

And all the other shit has cleared away.

Kate takes a sip of champagne, her eyes drifting closed. "Delicious," she murmurs, taking another small drink.

I rest my hand on her knee, my fingers skating up her thigh over her jeans. She settles back on the seat, no qualms at all with my touch.

If anything, her legs relax open, granting me access.

My cock stirs and the headache lessons. Or maybe I just don't care.

If I tried to fuck her, would she let me? She'd probably tell me it was a bad idea until I got my memory back.

Fuck that.

Deep in my bones, I know this is my woman.

"One more question..." I give her a one-sided smile, my eyes drifting down her gorgeous face, to the long column of her neck, over her amazing rack and then lower, over her flat stomach, to where my hand is an inch from her pussy.

"Yeah?"

"How's the sex?"

I feel the muscles of her thighs clench, her nipples instantly growing hard as her breath catches.

I watch her eyes dilate as the glass stops halfway to her mouth. Have I rendered her speechless?

Good.

Holding the hand with the champagne, I brush the glass out of the way as I lean in to give her a soft kiss.

She sighs into my mouth, her lips pliant under mine, as I go in for a second brush.

That was all I needed to know.

CHAPTER TWENTY-FOUR

KATE

LUKE'S KISS NOT ONLY FEELS as good as it always does... it's even better.

There is some depth that I don't understand. It's deeper, longer, more tender. He explores my mouth like it's the first time, only it's also like he loves me.

It's not new to me but...

All at once, I realize it's like the first time all over again for him.

I open to him even further, arching my neck to a better angle. As if he understands, his hand slides up my chest, wrapping around the side of my neck, his fingertips settling in my hair, his thumb resting on my jaw.

He licks at the inside of my mouth, like he can't get enough of my taste, and I return the kiss, melting into him.

It's everything I've ever yearned for.

So open and intimate.

The car stops, the engine cutting.

Luke slowly draws back, his hand still wrapped around my neck.

"Mr. Kincaid," the driver calls from outside the door. "We've arrived."

Luke reluctantly pulls away, his hand sliding down my arm to take my hand in his. "Where exactly have we arrived to?" he asks as the door swings open.

The driver steps back, looking confused. "Your house, sir."

I step out behind him, my jaw dropping. "Shut up."

Luke scratches his chin. "Why didn't you say so?"

"I assumed…" the driver's voice trails off as another man in a black suit approaches.

"Mr. Kincaid," the man says, gesturing toward the stairs, "I'm Mike Evans. Head of security here. Let's get you inside."

Luke narrows his gaze. "All right."

He takes my hand, following the man up the stairs. "We have a team around the premises to make certain the man who attacked you can't do it again."

I feel a moment's relief but Luke tenses. "How many cars do I have in the garage?"

"Cars?"

"For tinkering… how many?"

Mike's shoulders slump in obvious relief. "Two for tinkering, sir."

"And how many for driving?"

Mike turns away with a wince. "None."

"You're telling me that I don't go to the grocery store?"

Mike shakes his head. "Not usually. No. The staff can provide any food you need."

"And Mason. When does he arrive?"

"He doesn't, I'm afraid, though Mrs. Kincaid is here in Aspen."

"Which house is hers?"

Mike points down the street. "I believe Mr. Kincaid—the other Mr. Kincaid—has left her here so that she'll be safe."

Luke rumbles a noncommittal response as he steps into the house.

I know something is bothering him, but I wait to ask, as I stop in the entry and just stare. We're in a massive two-story space with giant wood beams and an impressive mahogany staircase.

I can see a large family room down the hall at the back of the house. Luke opens a door to the left, revealing a study. He pokes his head in, looks around, and then closes the door again.

Taking my hand, we start up the stairs, "Where are we going?" I whisper, looking back at Mike, who stands in the entry, watching our retreat.

"To the master bedroom," he hits the top of the stairs and pauses, looking left and then right before he chooses a direction. "Wherever that is."

I look too and spot a room at the end of the hall that has a set of double doors. He sees it too and we start down the hall.

I know he's chosen correctly, when he throws open the doors to reveal a massive bed that fills the back wall. Stepping inside, there is a bank of floor-to-ceiling windows with a view out to the mountains.

But Luke just keeps going, pulling me deeper into the room and to another door.

I gasp when he turns on the light for the bathroom. A giant soaking tub sits beneath more windows, a glass-doored shower taking up the end of the large room.

"How many heads do you think that shower has?"

His gaze flicks to it before he turns on the taps for the tub. "We'll shower after."

"After what?"

"Our bath."

That is my Luke. Bossy as hell. But I kick off my shoes. Nothing would make me happier than to lay against him skin to skin.

He turns and adjusts the taps, checking the water as I strip off my T-shirt, reaching for the buttons of my jeans.

He turns toward me, his eyes landing on my chest, his jaw going granite-hard, his gaze dark and unreadable.

I feel my cheeks flush, insecurity pulsing through me. "Was I… was I supposed to wait?"

"No." He stands up stripping off his T-shirt too. "I can't wait…"

My face flames. He's forgotten what I look like. Everything is new again. But it makes me feel a little embarrassed. "I don't get naked in front of men very often. It's new and..."

"If you think I'm judging, love, I'm not." And then he steps up in front of me, reaching to unclip my bra. The straps slide part way down my shoulders. He brushes them the rest of the way down my arms, as the cups fall away from my breasts.

"Christ," he mutters. "So fucking perfect."

I blush even deeper. "You said... you told me you like the color of my..." I swallow down a lump. "Nipples."

"Oh. I do," he answers, but he doesn't touch them. Instead, he skims his fingers along my collarbone. Goosepimples break out all over my skin.

It feels like he's seducing me in a way he didn't the first time. I want to ask, but his middle finger is gliding down my chest, sliding between my breasts.

They continue right down my belly, until they reach the button of my jeans.

I'm already panting, my nipples pebbled, and my back arching. He undoes the button and the zipper, grabbing the waist and shimmying the tight pants over my hips.

I wiggle to help him, and with a growl, he drops into a crouch.

My jeans are around my knees, only my underwear is covering me. He tips forward, running his nose over the fabric covering my pussy. "When's the last time we had sex?"

"This morning," I reply just before his tongue darts out, licking at my still-covered slit. My head tips back and my hands come to his hair.

"How often do we fuck?"

But he starts licking swirling his tongue, the fabric only making it even more erotic.

I'm pulling at his hair. "Like rabbits," I gasp.

He laughs at that, the sound vibrating through my aching pussy.

And then he pushes away, standing up.

I nearly cry out from the loss, but he's undoing his own jeans now. "Get in the tub."

I scramble to do as he's requested, wiggling the rest of the way out of my jeans and panties as I step in.

He's right behind me.

His arms come around me, his fingers diving between my folds.

I fall back into him, my hips jutting forward.

But he's not satisfied with the position, and he pulls me down into the water, flipping me over so my shoulder blades rest on the edge of the tub. "Lean back on the edge," he rumbles. I do as he commands, my arms resting and stretching out along the rim, as he lifts my hips with his hands.

And then he dives face-first into my pussy.

The water is warm as it laps at my body and his tongue is working me exactly where I need it. I try to relax and enjoy but he's a man on a mission, swirling over my clit with such precision that it takes less than a minute before I explode on his tongue.

He roars as he pushes up, turning me over again and thrusting into me from behind. "You cum so pretty," he growls out as he fills my insides, stretching me. "I want to hear it again."

And then he starts a relentless pace, his hand cupping my mound, his middle finger working my clit.

I try to grasp the edge of the tub as water sloshes onto the floor.

It's fast and hard and my body is vibrating to do exactly as he told me to. But I hold out, waiting for him as he pushes inside me over and over.

"Luke," I gasp, the effort of not cumming making me raw.

But he stops. "Sweetheart?" he sounds worried. "I'm not hurting you, am I?"

I look back over my shoulder, barely able to focus. "No. It's so good." It comes out in a broken sob.

He thrusts into me again, bending over my body. "You're mine, Kate. Mine to take care of. You tell me what you need, and I'll give it to you, baby."

"I need to cum," I cry, clawing at the side. "Please, Luke. Please."

He thrusts harder, the force of his hips setting off fireworks inside my body as I ripple around him and then break apart, crying with a force that shocks even me.

He follows right behind me, his roar fills my ears as he fills me with his cum.

I slump onto the edge of the tub, my eyes drifting closed. I've got to find a way to get birth control pills here.

Otherwise, our problems are only going to multiply.

Luke slumps across my back, kissing a trail down my spine. "Holy shit, love. That was…"

"I asked you a couple days ago if this was normal…"

"The sex? It's beyond special."

I look back at him. "Getting your memory back?"

He lifts his head and smiles back. "There are some things a man just knows."

The water in the tub is starting to cool, but I don't think I have the strength to get out. Luke stands and lifts me in his arms, carrying me into the shower and turning on multiple heads so that I'm doused in warm water.

He squirts body wash into his hand, scrubbing my skin until the tiredness begins to turn to need once again.

As my head tips back, I hear him rumble out his appreciation. "So that's how it is between us?"

"How's that?"

"We're a freight train of passion."

"We are," I look down as his hand slips between my legs.

That's when a knock sounds at the door. "Mr. Kincaid."

Luke's head snaps up, his eyes narrowing. "Yes?"

"Mr. Kincaid is on the phone, sir. He'd like to speak with you."

Luke stands, a rumble sounding from his chest. Pouring more bodywash into his hand, he starts washing himself.

"Umm…" I start. "Did you need…"

"I'll answer in a minute," Luke replies, his gaze swinging to me, his eyes softening. "You're all right if I take this call?"

My brows go up. This is an unexpected change. "Of course."

He scrubs himself, rinses off, and gets out of the shower. "I won't be long."

And then he steps out of the shower, leaving me to wash my hair.

Wrapping a towel around his waist, he steps out of the bathroom. I move as quickly as I can.

I'd like to hear this conversation.

CHAPTER TWENTY-FIVE

LUKE

TOWEL STILL HUNG around my hips, I walk out to my bedroom to find Mike waiting near the door.

I snatch the phone from his hand, as I glare. "Mike."

"Yeah?" he asks, his hands folding in front of him.

"You're fired."

He visibly starts. "But…"

"Get the fuck out of my bedroom."

He hesitates for a moment before he turns. I step into the hall, noting two more guards in the entry. "No one enters my bedroom without permission."

And then I walk back in, slamming the door.

"Luke?"

It's Mason, speaking through the phone.

"Yeah?" I'm not amused with my cousin. I'm certain he told Mike to interrupt me and I'm starting to think my hunch about being a partial prisoner here was correct.

"Mike was just following orders, I needed you—"

It's as I thought, but it doesn't make me feel any better. "This is my house?"

"Yes."

"Would you allow staff to enter your bedroom where your wife was naked?"

Mason pauses. "She's not your wife."

"Think of her like she is." I need him to understand this and I'm not backing down.

Another stretch of silence. "You've only been back to the house for twenty minutes."

"So?"

"You fucked her already."

"What the fuck?" I spit into the phone. "What business is it of yours?"

Mason rumbles, a sound of deep dissent. "We are family, Luke. We have each other's backs. We keep our word."

"And which part of my word meant that I screwed Kate over?"

Mason doesn't answer.

"I want to speak to Roman. I can actually remember him, and I need—"

"You can't speak to Roman, Luke." His voice gets deadly quiet.

Two can play that game. "Why not?"

More silence. "He doesn't know."

I stare at the phone as Kate comes out of the bathroom in a fluffy white towel. She looks beautiful and fragile. Her wide eyes tell me she's heard most of the conversation. Did she hear me refer to her as my wife?

She stops when our eyes meet, nipping at her lip.

"What do you mean Roman doesn't know? Know what?"

"Roman doesn't know you're alive."

Roman and Arabella are the most important people in the world to me besides Kate. "You better not mean what I think you mean."

Mason sighs. "We all have a part to play. He needs to keep focused and thinking…"

I growl into the phone. "What you actually mean is that you're manipulating him the way you are me."

"It's not like that, Luke. This tunnel is everything. I need—"

"Not to me, it's not. To me, my family is everything."

"But this is about family. This project makes us impenetrable. Safe."

I gesture Kate closer. I need to feel her skin.

She comes without question. "Set aside your ambitions for one fucking second, Mason, and tell me the truth. Having me ruin a woman's life, that's really how you want to do this? That's justifiable to you?"

"Providing for the safety of my family justifies nearly any means."

I grit my teeth together. "Tomorrow, Kate and I are leaving for New York. I won't show my face in Vegas, and I'll use cash. But she is getting another internship, and I won't remain hidden and ruin her future."

"You can't. I need—"

"Fuck you, Mason. It's not about you. It never was." I almost hang up but then I stop. "I'm calling Roman and Arabella tonight and then I'm leaving tomorrow. Try and stop me, and our split will not be amicable."

"Split? What the fuck are you talking about?"

"I'm selling my shares. I'm out." And then I hang up the phone.

Kate is front of me, tears shimmering in her eyes. "You don't need to quit, Luke, I..."

I pull her against me, kissing her mouth like I'll die if I don't.

I don't need to remember everything. I remember enough.

She melts into me, her arms threading around my neck. I'd like to lay her down and fuck her senseless, again.

"Go dry your hair, sweetheart," I say, against her lips. "If it's all right with you, I've got another call to make."

"Of course it's all right, but seriously, Luke. You didn't have to—"

"I promised you we were going to New York, baby. I told you I'm going to work on cars, maybe open a high-end shop. It suits me, doesn't it?"

"It does," she whispers.

"And you are going to get another internship. Finish med school."

She shakes her head, her eyes wide. "My mom would never in a million years believe this one."

"Would she be proud?" I remember her mom made a habit of dating really fucked up men…

And then I blink. Because a whole bunch of shit is just back in my brain. Wow. That's weird.

"Appalled. She'd surely make a crack about me ruining the meal ticket."

And then she kisses me again, her hands threading through my hair. "But I know you're the best kind of guy."

I slide my hand down her spine, seriously reconsidering that call. I just want to yank the towel off her and…

Then I remember the story she told me about her mom's deadbeat boyfriend who tried to hurt her. That guy is going to fucking pay.

"Dry your hair, love."

She kisses me two more times before disappearing into the bathroom again.

I hear the blow dryer turn on and then I pull on a pair of exercise pants and a T-shirt I find in the drawer. I throw another shirt of mine on the bed for Kate.

I head straight out the front door. Two security men turn toward me. "I'm still a Kincaid and my share is equal to Mason's. Try to stop me and you'll find yourself without a job," I bark and then exit the house.

This is a family compound and I head straight for the house that sits at the end of the street, looking down on all the others. Trotting up the steps, I ring the bell.

A housekeeper answers. "I need to speak with Charlotte."

"Of course, Mr. Kincaid," the housekeeper bobs a curtsy, making me instantly feel like shit.

"Thank you," I follow up, giving her a much softer smile.

Charlotte appears at the top of the stairs and a vision of her at her wedding fills my thoughts. A delicate brunette, I can't help but notice that she bears a resemblance to Kate. Do Mason and I share the same taste in women? Interesting.

The memories are coming back faster and faster. "Luke!" she cries, racing down the stairs. "What are you doing here?"

"It's a long story." I comb one hand through my hair. "But I need a favor."

"Anything."

"I need to speak with Arabella, but I don't have my phone. I'm shit with numbers."

She gives me a smile and pulls out her phone. She hits two buttons and the phone is ringing.

"Char?" I hear Arabella's voice and the tension in my shoulders unwinds.

"No, bug. It's me. Luke."

"Luke!" she cries. "It's been way too long."

"It has," I smile. "Listen. I'm going to New York for a while and before I go..."

"Are you visiting me?"

My brows lift and Charlotte gives me a quizzical stare. Right. Probably something I should have known. "Soon. I'm planning on staying for a while."

"What about Kincaid Enterprises?" she asks.

"I'll explain when I see you, but right now, I need a small favor. Can you call Roman and tell him I'm all right? He'll want to know."

"Sure," Ari's sweet voice fills the phone. "Of course I can."

"Thanks, bug," I say. "I love you."

"Okay, now you're just being weird."

That makes me smile. "I think I'm going to ask a woman to marry me."

Arabella squeals. "That's amazing. Do I get to be a bridesmaid again? Never mind. No pressure on your girl. I'm so happy for you."

Charlotte is smiling too, but Charlotte is Mason's wife, and she likely knows far more about what's going on, which means there is a tension in her eyes that her smile can't hide. I hang up with Arabella and hand Charlotte her phone back. "Listen. I could use some phone numbers, but Mason isn't going to like it."

"My husband will deal," she answers, taking my phone from me. "And I'll give you all the numbers you want after you explain. Who are you marrying and how did you end up here? Last time I heard, your blood was in the back of a car."

"Yeah." Then I take a deep breath. "Actually, Kate might do a better job of explaining than me. Want to meet her?"

Kate should start meeting my family and Mason might not understand the importance of winning over the female family members instead of screwing them over, but I sure as shit do.

"Of course, I do,"

"Warning, though. Mason has been a real prick to both of us."

Charlotte's mouth purses into a fine line. "He has been acting strangely since he went back to Vegas."

That is not my problem. Not right now.

Right now, I need to make sure that Kate gets to New York and to her future.

CHAPTER TWENTY-SIX

KATE

I WAKE TO THE SUNRISE, the first rays just lighting the room, as I stretch against Luke, his arms wrapped tight around me.

He tightens his arms, snuggling his nose into the crown of my hair. "Good morning," he murmurs.

I smile burrowing deeper. "Good morning."

"Read for our road trip?"

I sigh. Maybe.

I appreciate what he's doing. I really do. He's trying to give me what I need and that is amazing.

But I heard him talking to Charlotte yesterday. This is his family. The kind I always wanted.

Even Mason… he was trying to protect his. I heard that and unlike every other conversation, I could hear the sincerity in his voice when he talked about keeping the family safe.

Luke doesn't remember that now, but how will he feel when all his memories come back and I'm the person who caused the rift, pulled him away from the people he loves?

Besides, between losing that internship and meeting Luke, I'm suddenly questioning my choices. If I could take away the assumption that I had to be great, what would I be? What would I do?

I shake my head. "I don't think—"

"You're not giving up your future for a tunnel."

I turn in his arms, wanting to see his face. "You're not giving up your family for my PhD."

He grimaces but he still cups my ass, pulling my pelvis into the cradle of his. "I'm not giving up Roman. Or Arabella."

"Call Roman first, at least," I whisper sliding my arms around his neck. "Get his take on all of this since you trust him."

Luke gives a tentative nod, pushing up from the bed.

"How many days will the trip take?" I ask as he pulls a pair of workout pants over his muscular legs and over his narrow hips.

"Three," he answers, rummaging for the phone.

"I'm going to call my advisor. See what opportunities she might have and when they start. See if we can stay—"

"I don't want to stay," he shakes his head. "It doesn't feel right here."

My brows lift. "The shower felt pretty good. So did the bath."

He looks back at me with that one-sided grin that always steals my breath. Then he picks up the phone. He pushes a few buttons and starts for the door.

I push up too, grabbing his discarded shirt. Once again, I have no clothes.

Charlotte let me borrow some stuff, but I can't wait until we're settled in one place.

What a crazy ride this has been.

Distantly, I hear Luke's voice. Did Roman pick up or is he leaving a voicemail? Stretching, I start for the bathroom.

I can at least brush my teeth and my hair before Luke comes back up.

A noise just outside the bedroom door makes me turn. "Done already?" I ask, concern knitting my brow.

No one answers.

Shaking my head, I continue into the bathroom, running the

toothbrush under the water and then placing some toothpaste on the brush before I start brushing.

Spitting, I bend down to wash my face in cool water. It's loud enough that I almost miss the low whistle.

I shut off the water, scrubbing my face. "Hand me a towel, would you?"

"Towel?"

The voice makes me stop cold. That is not Luke.

Spinning, I gasp in a breath. Guerriero stands in the bathroom door looking at me like I'm some kind of snack and he's starving.

I take a step back, bumping into the countertop. I try to scream but no sound comes out.

His eyes run up and down me, the only thing covering my body… Luke's T-shirt.

"Luke," it comes out a hoarse whisper. But then I get it out a second time, louder. "Luke!"

Guerriero gives me a wick smile. "No use."

I tear my gaze from his, long enough to see the glass jar full of cotton balls on the counter.

Not giving myself a chance to change my mind, I pick it up and throw it at Guerriero. He easily deflects it, but it crashes to the tile floor, smashing into a thousand tiny pieces.

Was it loud enough?

I hope so. Because I'm in bare feet and the floor is now covered in glass…

Guerriero keeps walking. When he's close enough, I try to dart around him but it's no use.

He reaches out a hand, grabbing my arm, the other wrapping around my throat.

My eyes go wide as he squeezes. "You big problem."

"Me?" I gasp out. "You."

He gives me another cold smile. "I big. Yes."

Is he talking about what I think he is? I don't have a chance to be upset, I'm too busy trying to breathe as he squeezes harder.

My eyes bulge as I try to breathe but I'm losing, and my knees weaken as I sink to the floor.

"Sleep," he whispers leaning close. "When you wake we've got—"

But he doesn't finish.

I catch a flash before Luke is on him, snapping the man's head back.

I hear a crack before the hand at my throat goes limp. I don't have a chance to be relieved as I collapse into a heap, gasping for breath. Luke scoops me into his arms, carrying me across the glass. I can't even imagine what I look like.

"Is he dead?" I croak out.

"No," Luke whispers against my temple, even as security personnel flood into the room.

"I'm so sorry," one of them skids to a stop as the rest flood into the bathroom. "He knocked out one of the men on the perimeter. Scaled the balcony." He points to the open French door.

Luke gently sets me on the bed and tosses a blanket over me, then turns back and whispers to the men.

I have no idea what he's saying, and I don't care.

Gently, I feel my own throat, testing for swelling, swallowing to assess the damage. Bruising only, I think.

The phone rings but Luke doesn't answer. Instead, his weight settles on the bed next to me. "Just keep the covers over your face for a few more seconds, love, and then we can check you over."

"I'm fine," I rasp out, my voice hoarse.

His hand settles on my hip. I hear the room clear and then he pulls the covers off of me.

I turn even as his eyes scan down me. "Fuck," he rumbles as he looks at my neck.

I shake my head. "He wasn't going for the kill. He was just trying to make me black out. The damage is minimal."

"It doesn't fucking look minimal," he grits out.

"What happened to him? Gorilla?"

"Let me worry about him."

The phone rings again. Luke looks down at it, his eyes flickering before he dismisses the call.

But it just rings again. I close my eyes. "Pick up."

A moment of indecision fills his eyes before he answers. "Roman."

"You're fucking alive."

I smile. Roman sounds just like Luke.

"I'm alive. Though Guerriero just tried pretty fucking hard to end Kate."

"Fuck," Roman rumbles. "She all right?"

"Still checking."

"Vincent and Vigo got bailed out yesterday. Came after us last night. We're all right, but they're both dead."

Luke's shoulders sage. "Thank fuck."

Our gazes lock. If all three of the Vendettis are out of the picture...

"Roman. I think I might be out. I'll explain it all later, but I'm not sure I want to work for Kincaid anymore."

Roman pauses for a moment. "That's funny. I've been thinking the same thing."

He touches my cheek, giving me a soft smile as he finishes his call.

Then his fingertips skim down my jaw to my throat, assessing my neck. "I'm fine, Luke. Promise."

He leans down and places a soft kiss on the column of my throat. "As soon as you're up for it, let's call your advisor. Where do you want to go?"

That is an excellent question.

CHAPTER TWENTY-SEVEN

Kate

I chew on my nail as the phone in my hand rings. I'm waiting for my advisor to pick up as I stand inside the small Durango hangar.

We flew back this morning. Back to the cabin and to Alice.

First, I wanted the clothes that Luke bought for me. Second… he wants the truck. He says he's going to have it towed back to Vegas for now, while we're figuring out where we want to land.

I know he had this plan to go back to New York, but where we go depends on where there is an open internship. This late, I have no idea where or if I'll be able to find one.

Which is why this call is so important. But on a more personal note, and the last reason we're here…

I want Mark to meet Luke.

This is my way of making things official.

My advisor picks up. "Hello?"

"Hi Doctor McCabe. It's Kate Adams."

"Kate! You sound awful. Are you all right?"

I give a slight smile. Did Gorilla do me a small favor? I probably sound like I've got the flu with the rasp in my voice. "I'll survive. But I did miss the start of my internship, and I don't think the attending researcher was very pleased."

"I heard. He called me and I told him again what I said when I recommended you. You have the highest work ethic of any of my students. I know for a fact you would have been there if there wasn't an emergency."

Her words untwist a knot in my stomach. One doctor can think I'm a flake. I should have known Dr. McCabe would have my back. Then again, I'm not used to people supporting me. "Thank you so much for that. It's so appreciated. But now I find myself without an internship."

"Hmm," she says, and I can hear her clicking buttons. "I've got a few left here in New York, but honestly, they are kind of the bottom of the barrel. One research position in a STEM lab. One position at the New York City Hospital."

I wrinkle my nose. Neither suit me, and both are across the country. I'd like to give Luke time to collect all his memories and figure out stuff with his family.

"I do have one in Las Vegas, since you're already there. But it's with a pediatrician, which I know is not your preferred specialty."

My heart soars. "Actually, that sounds perfect."

Pediatricians do not make big money. I have no idea how I'll pay off my loans, but working with kids feels so right. I want to be a doctor. I want to help people. But I don't feel the same need to prove my worth to the world. I just want to be me.

"Really? I thought you wanted to go into surgery?"

I draw in a deep breath. "Vegas has been… enlightening."

My gaze catches on Luke, who watches Mark pull up in Alice. Mark gets out of the truck and the two shake hands. They barely speak three words before they're lifting the hood of the car.

My mouth hangs open for a second before a giant, and probably goofy smile, splits my face. I didn't even realize how much I wanted them to like each other.

I focus back in on the call. "I can't wait to hear all about it. The start date for the pediatrician office is listed as flexible. Should I call them?"

"Yes, please. Thank you so much."

We hang up. As much as I'd like to rush to Mark's side, I hang back. I give the man who helped me know how to pick a good man when I found him a chance to meet Luke and see what I see.

He's the best kind of man there is.

Watching Luke and Mark fills my heart.

CHAPTER TWENTY-EIGHT

Luke

I like Mark right away. He's a good dude.

First, he replaced Alice's starter for me, and she's purring like a kitten. We talk about trucks for a minute, before he turns to me. "Gotta ask. What are your intentions toward Kate?"

I like a man who gets right to the point. And I like that he's got my girl's interests at heart too. "The best," I answer. "Kate is an amazing woman."

He quirks a brow but doesn't ask me to elaborate. Which is good. Because I'm not sure telling him that I'd like to propose after a week of dating makes me look good. I might sound crazy.

Maybe I am.

But I've got another topic we need to discuss. "Look, I know we just met, and I know this is sensitive, but I've got a question too."

"Shoot."

"That guy that hurt Kate in high school…"

"She told you about that?" he asks. "She tell you what happened?"

"Yes. She did."

"Is it as bad as I always thought?"

"Yeah. It's pretty bad."

His fists clench around the rag he's holding. "Damn it."

Again, I don't want Mark to think I'm crazy. "You got an address for this guy? I'd like to chat with him."

Mark clears his throat. "I do, but he's going to be tough to talk to."

I cock my head. "Why's that?"

"He resides in a cemetery."

I don't ask and Mark doesn't say, but something tells me Mark might have helped put the guy there. And if that's the case, we've got even more in common than I thought. "Good to know."

Kate comes over, beaming at us. "I got another internship!"

"That's great, sweetheart," I smile back, wrapping my arm around her shoulders. I give her a quick kiss on the forehead before I let her go again so she can greet Mark.

I give them a minute before I ask the question. "So where are we taking Alice? Back to New York?"

She nips at a lip, a sure sign she's not sure of my reaction. "Not exactly."

"Where?"

"It's in Vegas."

I frown, but don't answer in front of Mark. It's the only place I don't think I want to go. But I'll do anything for Kate.

And she's got it in her head that she shouldn't separate me from family. I get what she's saying, but my priorities are right in line. Kate first. Arabella and Roman second. Kincaid Enterprises… never again.

Which becomes even more obvious when my phone rings. Arabella's name pops up. "Can you two give me a second? It's my sister."

"Of course," Kate nods and smiles. "Tell Arabella I said hello."

Mark smiles too. With a quick nod of thanks to them both, I turn to answer the phone. "Hey, bug. Everything all right?"

"Not really," she huffs. "Mason just called. He says I have to come to Vegas for the rest of the summer."

Mason.

I know that he's Ari's benefactor, but if he thinks he's going to mess with her life, he's got another thing coming.

Me and him. We'll have to go some rounds.

"Why is that?"

Arabella is quiet for a moment. "I didn't want to rain on your news about Kate, but I've been seeing this guy…"

My hackles go up. "Yeah?"

"And Mason says that I'm going to get some shares and then Preston proposed and now I'm all confused…"

My fist clenches at my side. This does not sound good. Not at all.

Kate gives me a quizzical look, surely wondering abut the dark expression on my face.

More and more memories are filtering back. And I know if I'm taking on Mason, I'm going to need some help.

Maybe being in Vegas for the summer is a good thing after all. Kate's right. There is some shit to work out with my family, I just don't think it's in the way Kate's envisioning.

"You can stay with me and Kate, bug. You're going to love her."

"Thank you," Arabella answers. "But Mason already set me up in one of the apartment complexes, so I'd have a place of my own. Which is a shitty consolation prize. I just landed a position at Dior that I'm going to have to give up. I could kill Mason."

"There is a lot of that going around." I'm going to have to talk to Roman. It might be time to do something about our leader.

EPILOGUE

Six months later...

Kate

"Almost ready?" Luke calls from the bedroom.

It's nearly Christmas and we're staying at Luke's Vegas apartment while we're in the city to celebrate the holidays with his family and attend Arabella's wedding.

I check the loose waves of my hair, made even prettier by the stylist who left fifteen minutes ago. "Almost."

Luke appears in the door just as I pull on the pale pink gown I'm wearing.

His eyes darken. "I should have stayed in the bedroom," he rumbles. "I just want to take that dress back off you."

I blush. Inwardly I heat too, because I am very much looking forward to when he peels this dress off of me and we do all manner of deliciously dirty things.

But right now... "Arabella will kill us both if we're late."

"Bug would. You're right."

"Zip me," I say, pointing to my back.

He pushes off the door jam and saunters into the bathroom. "It's bad enough that I have to look at you like this, dressed in the perfect shade to match your gorgeous nipples, but now you want me to touch you?"

I roll my eyes. "You'll control yourself somehow."

He grabs my zipper and slowly pulls the dress closed, kissing my shoulder as he does. "You overestimate my control."

I tip my head, giving him more access to my neck. I overestimate my own too. One more kiss and I might rip the dress off myself.

Reaching for the small jewelry holder, I slip my engagement ring on my finger. The stunning pink diamond shimmers back up at me. "The dress matches my ring."

Luke's arm snakes around my body, his fingers splaying out over my belly. "Don't crinkle the silk," I whisper even as my ass settles against his already hard cock.

"Oh, I'm going to mess you up so good," he rumbles into my ear. "Wrinkled. Stained. Mussed." His tongue is swirling up my neck. "Might have to do it right now."

"Luke," I gasp, pushing closer. "After all the work and money…" The stylist alone must have cost a small fortune.

I'm slowly adjusting to the fact that Luke is ridiculously rich and likes spending money on me.

Even with everything that's happened with Mason, he has enough money that I'm not sure we could spend it all in multiple lifetimes.

"That's what money is for."

"To make me so beautiful that you can't resist making a mess of me?"

"You don't need money to make you more beautiful. You're stunning. It's just more fun to mess what's been painstakingly organized."

I roll my eyes as he slides his hand lower. Even knowing we need to leave, my core tightens, the tingle of desire spreading through me.

That's when his phone rings.

He lets out a sigh and takes a step back. "You've been saved," he chuckles as he picks up the phone. "Hey, Roman. Everything good?"

Roman and Maddie are about to get married too. They've been delaying because they're building a shelter for wounded animals. It's going to be a nonprofit division for Kincaid, with Roman splitting duties between Kincaid and his passion project.

We're the only ones who don't have a date for our wedding. Luke says he doesn't care when or how we do it, just so long as I'm wearing the engagement ring so that other men know I'm claimed.

I shake my head every time he says it. Men are not banging down my door. But I like that he's worried they might.

I focus back on my fiancé, who is scowling like something is seriously wrong.

"What?" I mouth, worry skittering through me.

Our lives are pretty normal in New York. I go to school. Luke has started a new business refurbishing old cars.

Not only is he great at it, he's already turning a hefty profit… I know because I keep his books. But I think he'd work on cars even if he made no money. He's so happy doing it.

I can feel it. He's excited to get up every day and go to work.

And I feel that way too.

Working with the pediatrician this summer was a revelation. I can't wait to get started on my career.

But every time we come back to Vegas, we get pulled into Luke's old life.

He hangs up the phone. "Arabella sat us with Mason and Charlotte," Luke growls. "I know she wants us to make up."

I give him an encouraging smile. I agree. Mason made the wrong choices. But he had a lot of valid reasons for them.

Even I can see that.

And if I'm honest, missing that internship has turned out to be one of the best mistakes of my life.

But Luke isn't just mad about that. He's also upset about everything that's happened with Arabella over the last six months…

"Smile and be nice," I say, applying a little more gloss on my lips before I pass Luke to collect my clutch from the bed.

"I don't want to play nice. I want to bash in his face."

Professionally, they've mostly worked things out. Personally, it's a different story. Charlotte says that the boys just fall out from time to time. A hazard of so many alphas in the same space.

And I have intimate knowledge of what a jerk Mason can be. But deep down, I think his heart is the right place. So I offer up a compromise.

I look back at Luke, cocking my head. "I'll make you a deal… be civil and I'll blow you halfway through the reception."

Luke pauses, cocking his head. "Your blowjobs are the best."

I give him an encouraging smile. "So you'll be civil?"

He makes a noncommittal sound. "I'll be civil cause I know you want my family to be yours too. But I'll take the blowjob."

I step up to him and kiss his cheek, leaving a kiss mark on it. "Thank you. Now let's go before we're late. I've got bridesmaid duties to attend."

"I love you, sweetheart." He kisses my lips, getting more of my gloss on him. "You're my shotgun, ride or die, baby."

"You're mine too," I give him a smile. "You, me, Alice until the end."

He laughs at that.

"Can you imagine how the real Alice reacted when Clyde opened up my check?"

"Think he got a blowjob too?" I say with a laugh.

He pulls me close. "Do I need to make you cum so that you forget any other man exists?"

I shake my head. "Luke, you know you're the only man for me."

"That's right, love." He kisses me again and I swear, he's wearing more of my gloss than I am before he finally pulls away and takes my hand. "Let's do this."

We leave the bedroom and head toward the elevator. "I've been thinking about it. Want to just get married at the cabin this summer?"

He stops again, the glint in his eyes electric. "Abso-fucking-lutely."

My hand in his, the elevator doors open and we step inside. It's time to focus on Arabella.

She's earned it…

WOW!!!! The Kincaids have been the most amazing family!!

One more book left. Keep reading to find out what happens to Arabella and how she brings the Kincaid clan back together!!! Turn the page for a sneak peek of, *King of Deception*!

King of Deception

A POWERFULLY CUNNING **billionaire**
A sacrificial mafia princess

I might have had one too many glasses of champagne.
It's the hazard of toasting a wedding that feels like a life sentence.

But when I stumble across the lawn of the oceanside hotel, I mistake the wrong set of open French doors for my own.

AND RUN smack into the most sinfully delicious man I've ever laid eyes on...

Gris Smith looks like a dream.
Gorgeous.
Sexy.
And the accent.

It doesn't matter that I'm a virgin.
Or that my family's business is at stake.

My clothes join his on the bathroom floor.
It's hotter than I ever imagined.
But it's meant to be a single night. One indulgence before I give myself over to duty.

The problem, though?
Gris isn't a dream. He's a nightmare.
The devil in disguise.

Because he isn't just some random stranger.
He is my family's greatest enemy.

He knows exactly who I am.

Exactly how to use me to take everything my family has built.

AND I WALKED RIGHT into his trap.

KING OF DECEPTION

Arabella

I step away from the circle of light surrounding the beachside bar and draw a deep breath of ocean air as the darkness surrounds me.

Finally, I can breathe.

I'd normally find an oceanside resort on the island of Maui fun, if not relaxing. But not this time.

"Bella, come back!" Cici calls from her stool on the bar. "We've just started!"

"You go ahead," I call back to Cici and Maggie who already have several men circling. They'll have more fun without me. "Put your drinks on Mason's tab."

My champagne flute is still in my hand. I'm not much of a drinker, and I think this might be my third.

My friends kept ordering them for me. I didn't have the heart to tell them, the last thing I feel like doing is celebrating.

The diamond on my finger catches a bit of light from the nearby beachside bungalows, making the stone sparkle, further mocking me and my mood.

What would happen if I twisted the three-carat monstrosity off my finger and tossed it into the ocean?

My fiancé would likely just buy me another. The ring is, for sure, insured. He's not the sort of man who leaves anything to chance.

Preston Wingate III is the kind of old money that makes my family look like hustlers. Technically, we are.

My father was a gangster. My brothers try to hide it from me, but I know the truth. He worked for the Italian Mafia until it killed him.

And I actually mean killed him. He was murdered by a mob boss, Toni Carcetti.

It's why I've stayed away from the family and the business. I turned eighteen, went off to college, and I almost never come home.

It's a shit thing for me to have done. My oldest brother, Mason Kincaid, has turned us legitimate. He's a real estate phenom, owning and building half the Las Vegas strip and the hotels, condos, and luxury clubs that support it.

But the danger has always felt a breath away.

And my brothers can't hide the fact that all of them are still gangsters.

They're not telling me everything, but I think this last summer, that danger exploded. And now, my brother Roman and my cousin-like-a-brother, Luke, are no longer speaking to Mason.

And Luke is selling his shares.

Mason's buying them, of course. He never misses a business trick. But in a twist I didn't see coming, he's putting them in my name. Something about needing to diversify shares for the board. I don't know.

My defection from the family has come to an end. I've been drawn right back into the web.

It's a place I never wished to be.

And that's when I met Preston. Handsome. Charming. He's everything I should want. And best of all, he's old money, the kind with names and connections.

I stumble as I cross the lawn. Each beachside bungalow has sweeping water views, each cute and posh, but all looking exactly alike. I pause for a moment. Which one was mine? Third over? Or was it the fourth?

Drawing in a deep breath, I start forward again. I'm not worried. I left my French doors open, no one in a place like this steals from an unlocked room.

But it also means all the other guests have left their doors open too.

Stopping, I scrunch my brows and search the cute little buildings with their front porches and steps right into the sand.

I was the third... I'm sure of it.

Swallowing down my last bit of champagne, I start up the two steps and set my glass down on the porch table. I slip my heels off the moment I reach the top of the stairs.

I reach down and grab the straps, so they're dangling from a finger as I make my way inside.

A single small lamp by the bed is on, and I don't bother to turn on more as I move to the dresser, dropping my shoes.

I see my black suitcase in the corner, just where I left it.

I slip off my earrings, setting them on top of the entertainment console, then do the same with the monster ring.

A sigh escapes my lips to have the thing off. I'd rethink my decision to marry Preston, but I don't even know how to start the conversation.

When he asked, part of me was relieved. I didn't want to be in the business. Preston could handle it for me. And then there is Mason. He's beyond thrilled to welcome Preston into the fold.

My fiancé brings us a legitimacy that Mason has always wanted, and further protection from our enemies. Mason has already started attending the country club events with Preston and has possible deals with several of Preston's friends.

I shake my head, my eyes sliding closed. Everything started happening so fast... before I knew it, invitations were being sent out, and dresses were being picked and...

I'm not sure Preston loves me any more than I love him. What he has in connections, I have in money. Something he's been lacking of late. Not that you'd know it by his lifestyle.

But at twenty-two, this isn't how I saw my life going.

I was studying fashion in New York, talking about getting a job with a designer, working my way up the corporate ladder.

But there is no going back now.

Unclipping my bracelet watch that Luke gave me for Christmas, I turn toward the bathroom. My head is spinning and all I want to do is fall asleep.

But that's when I realize the bathroom light is on. Did I leave it on? Cocking my head, I pull my dark brown hair over one shoulder, reaching the zipper at the back of my dress.

I just want to brush my teeth and collapse into bed.

But when I reach for the bathroom door, it's locked. I blink a few times, trying to understand, when the look clicks and the door swings open.

I gasp, taking a step back, my eyes going wide.

Standing before me, backlit, is a nearly naked man. The light highlights the glistening breadth of his shoulders, the narrow taper of his waist, the long, lean length of him.

Taking another step back, a squeaking scream tumbles from my lips.

He steps out of the bathroom, the towel around his hips, slung low enough that I can see the cut of his muscle at his hip.

Because all the light is behind him, I can't make out his face, but he can see mine. I start to scream again, my hands coming to my face.

He straightens. "Usually people who break into other people's rooms aren't the ones who look so frightened or the ones who scream."

My mouth drops open as it takes me at least three seconds longer than it should to process those words. Maybe it's the posh British accent that slows my understanding, or maybe it's the champagne, but suddenly I realize, I'm in the wrong room!

Spinning, I bump right into the bed, my shin clonking the frame as I gasp out in pain.

I'm skittering to the side, my face flaming as I half hop and nearly trip in my effort to collect my things.

"I'm so sorry—" I start and this time, really trip over my own shoes.

I feel myself falling but I'm too intoxicated to stop myself. But that's the exact moment that strong arms circle my torso and suddenly, I stop halfway to the floor, my front pressed to a rock-hard chest.

My eyes go wide as my hand bites into flexing biceps. I mean… wow.

My chin snaps up and I'm looking into the dark brown depths of the most sinfully beautiful eyes I've ever seen. Or maybe it's just his whole face.

Straight nose, strong cheekbones, a jaw that could cut glass. The only thing soft is his mouth and my God, heat floods between my legs as I stare at that mouth. I'd like for those lips to devour me.

Wait. How long have we been like this, suspended halfway between standing and the floor? "I… I'm… I'm so sorry," I rasp out, my voice taking on this sultry tone I've never heard before. "I'll just get my things and…"

He quirks a half smile as his hands spread out on my back. Is he tired, holding me like this?

He doesn't seem it, his features completely relaxed. "Or…" The smile grows. "You could stay."

My mouth drops open. Did he just offer to… to… I can't even complete the thought.

I don't date.

It's part of having brothers who are always worried about my safety. That whole enemy thing.

In New York, I have a security detail. So I've never done a one-night stand before. I've never done anything before.

"I couldn't," I whisper, my mouth dry, my hands digging deeper into his skin like they're in complete revolt of my words. They don't seem to want to let him go.

He slowly pulls me to standing, but he doesn't let me out of his embrace. If anything, one of his hands slide lower, to the place just above my ass, pressing the cradle of my hips deeper into his. The ache between my legs gives a throb.

"Suit yourself," he murmurs, his mouth moving closer to mine. My eyes flutter closed. "Name's Gris."

"Bella," I answer, my fingers on my left hand unlock enough to slide up his arm until they reach his shoulder, my thumb settling in the deep cut of his collarbone.

"Nice to meet you, Bella," he replies and then his lips brush over mine in this featherlight kiss that is so soft, I wonder if I dreamed it.

"You too?" I return, my eyes still closed. When they finally open, I realize he's straightened up and I feel heat completely flood my cheeks. His hands slide to my sides and then trace down over the curve of my hips as he lowers himself into a crouch.

The towel parts revealing most of his thigh and I can almost see his… even as his head just in front of my…

I'm already aching between the legs, but at the proximity of his mouth, I feel the flood of moisture and I can actually smell my arousal in the air.

Which means he can smell me too. He looks up at me with another wicked grin before he grabs my shoes and stands back up.

My hands are on both his shoulders now. When did I reach for him with my other hand? I couldn't bring myself to stop touching him, apparently. He places the strappy three-inch sandals between us. "You'll need these then."

"Right," I say with a tiny nod. *Get it together, Arabella,* I chastise myself, as I let go of one of his shoulders and reach for the shoes, our fingers brushing.

I just need to collect up my things, slink out the door, die of embarrassment, and then figure out how to use the showerhead in my own room to relieve the ache between my legs.

But as I take the shoes, I look down and see the sparkle of the ring on his console. D color, VS1 quality in a platinum setting, it's perfectly cold and the idea of putting it back on my finger, makes me shiver.

Then I look back up at the man that I'm still holding with one hand. "What are the rules if I did stay?"

Oh, the way he looks at me. It's sin and I want to dive into it. "What do you want them to be?"

He isn't serious? I swallow down a lump. He's very serious.

"I…" I lick my lips and he watches the path of my tongue, his dark brown eyes growing even darker. "I can't have sex with you."

One of his brows quirks up. Does he know it's because I have another guy? The ring is right there…. I bet he hasn't guessed that it's because I've never done this. And I don't just mean the one-night stand.

I've never done any of it. I've never had sex before.

"Kissing?" he asks, his voice dropping low with the kind of heat that has me getting even wetter.

"Yes," I gasp a moment before he leans in, taking my mouth in a much firmer and deliberate press of his lips.

"How about here?" And then he bends a bit to place his lips on the fluttering pulse of my neck.

"Yes."

"Here?" he asks, planting another full-mouthed kiss in the middle of my chest.

My head tips back. "Yes."

His hands come to my zipper, the slow slide ringing in my ears. I'm not really big-chested, but I'm not small either. A solid C cup with breasts that are high and perky so I can go without a bra if the dress is right.

Which I did tonight.

The fabric of my cotton eyelet dress pools around my waist as he drops lower, his lips hovering just over one of my nipples. I can feel his warm breath on it, the proximity of his lips already making my nipple pucker. "Here?"

My head tips further back as I arch my chest up.

"Yes."

He sucks one nipple between his lips, his tongue swirling over the puckering skin and I cry out, burying my hands in his hair. I've never been the most sexual person. It honestly scared me.

But with him…

It's like he flipped some switch.

But he isn't done, not even close. He moves to the other breast, giving it equal attention before he slides lower. "Here?"

"Yes."

He licks at the skin of my stomach, tonguing my belly button before he tugs the dress lower, until it clears my hips and pools on the floor.

I'm only in my thong and I might be embarrassed but he stops his mouth an inch from the V between my legs. "Here?"

Even the idea of him kissing me where I ache has me sighing out a moan. "Yes." The way I say it, I might as well be begging.

If he stopped now, I'm pretty sure I would.

KING OF DECEPTION

Arabella

Fortunately for me, Gris doesn't stop. He tips forward the slightest bit and plants a kiss right on my sensitive clit, still covered in my thong, as another moan falls from my lips.

His tongue slides over the fabric and I hold onto his hair the way a cowgirl might hold the mane of a horse.

The strands are still damp from his shower, his cologne and natural woodsy scent filling my nostrils as I try to keep from whimpering out my begging pleas.

Hooking one of my legs over his shoulder, he places another kiss right where I need it most and then sucks on my clit.

It's like liquid fire shoots through me.

I had no idea that one man could turn me into this. Melt all my inhibitions in a matter of seconds, but here I am.

The ache pulses through me and I flex my hips to give him even more access. I don't want him to stop.

But he's done asking me what I want as he stands.

I cry out my protest anyway, even as he wraps an arm around my waist and lifts me up off the floor.

I've never felt my skin pressed to another man's skin like this before and it's amazing, the warm roughness of his skin against mine.

I wrap my arms around his neck, and he uses his other hand to tip my head down so that he can kiss my lips.

Using his mouth, he guides my lips apart, his tongue plunging into mine.

It's hot and sexy as our tongues tangle. I'm not so naïve that I've never kissed a man before. But I have never kissed like this. I can feel the heat between my legs spiraling out of control just from the press of our bodies and his kiss.

I don't even notice he's carrying me until he lowers me to the bed. If I thought his skin felt good when he carried me, when his weight comes down on top of me, I let out this long keening moan.

He's turned me into the most wanton woman…

But he's kissing down my body again and this time, when he gets to my belly, he fists either side of my thong, pulling it down over my hips.

I have one moment where I know he's going to see what no man has before, but I can barely think about it, before his lips come down over my clit and he sucks it into his mouth. Without the cloth, it feels even better, though it's sensitive enough that I bite at my lip, a little bit of pain mixing with the pleasure.

But he isn't done. He hooks a hand under my knee, opening me wider to him before his hand slides up my thigh, and then he uses his fingers to spread my other lips open.

The way he's touching me, confident, in command, it just makes me hotter as I chase his tongue with my hips.

And then he slides a finger inside me. I feel myself tighten around him. Grip him. But he feels so good inside me, my back arches, my hair sliding on the bed as I make this high-pitched cry.

He eases back, and my chin snaps down to look at him, about to beg for his touch. The look in his eyes makes my breath catch. It's so possessive it's almost predatorial.

"You like that, luv?"

"Please," I plead, my fingers sliding into his hair again. "Please don't stop."

He looks me at me for one more second, and I swear, he's like a lion about to devour his prey before he dives back in, licking me exactly where I need it.

I feel the pleasure knotting so tight that my back arches again, my toes curling, one fist clenching in the sheets, the other in his hair.

And then I break apart, shattering into a thousand tiny pieces as I cry out his name.

He slows his tongue but doesn't stop, his finger still buried inside me. My chest is heaving and I'm not sure I can see straight but I can still feel as he starts kissing a path back up my body.

But he doesn't remove his finger from inside me, his palm cupping my sex.

"In this arrangement of ours…" he growls out, his smooth accent making my inside walls clench around him again. "Do you return the favor?"

I lick my lips, drawing in a deep breath. Do I want to taste him? Feel him? "Yes."

I hear his rumble of approval a moment before my body is turning. He both pulls me on my side and spins me, so I'm lined up with my mouth pointed toward his hips where he crouches.

All while never taking his finger out of me.

The man has skills.

If I was ever going to do this… have one night of wild passion, I picked the right guy. It's so easy, I barely have to think.

With his free hand, he gives the towel a quick jerk and suddenly his cock is there in front of me.

My lips part as my eyes grow wide. Maybe I should have inspected the goods before I committed to the blowjob. I'm at the beginner level and even I know he is not beginner-sized.

He must sense my hesitation. With one hand still cupping between my legs, his finger inside me, he wraps a hand around the back of my head, his fingers sliding into my curtain of hair.

Slowly, he pulls me closer, and I lick my lips before I part them, letting the tip slide into my mouth.

My tongue darts out and I taste the smallest pearl of salty liquid. I've heard girls say it's gross, but I find it… kind of amazing.

I don't think delicious is the right word, but for some reason, I want more. It's just like him. Strong. Masculine. I sink my lips further down him, tentatively exploring.

"You ever done this before, Bella?"

I wince, knowing that he can tell. But he doesn't look upset as he pushes deeper into my mouth.

If anything, the cords of his neck stand out as he fists my hair tighter. I like that too. I think I would let this man do all manner of dirty things to me and that thought makes me sink even further, my lips wrapped around him until he hits the back of my throat.

And then, I don't know why, I hold. I like him filling me. I swear, I want to let him fill other places, not just my mouth.

We've barely started and his groan of approval, his head falling back, before he pulls my hair to slide his cock back out of my mouth. I come off with a pop, a little drool connecting my lip to the tip.

"Just like that," he grunts, pushing back into my mouth. "You're a natural."

Is he just saying that? I forget to worry as he hits the back of my throat again. "Hollow out your cheeks."

Is it weird that he's teaching me to do this?

But I do as he commands, letting him guide me with his hand at the back of my head.

His left hand is flexing against my scalp, his right still cupping my sex, his finger inside me. I can feel his body tightening, his cock lengthening and thickening in my mouth.

I swear, it's making me hotter, and my body is rising to meet his. My hips start rocking against his hand as I tighten around his finger.

"Fuck, Bella," he growls, pumping in and out of me. "You're so tight."

I sink even further down him, tears starting to stream from my eyes as I take as much of him in as I can.

It's like I can't get enough. I think I'm trying to take as much of him as possible while I have this chance.

I know what this is, Gris is not my Prince Charming. Just like I know what waits for me back home. But in this moment, I want as much of him as I can get.

I feel the current of energy that runs through him, I know he's close. I'm getting close too, my body beginning to shake as my second orgasm grows and swells.

I close my eyes, sliding up and down his thick shaft until he explodes in my mouth. I swallow him down, too far gone to even care, as my own body erupts in another orgasm.

I can't even cry out, but my eyes roll back, my body shuddering.

He pulls out of my mouth, his lips crashing down over mine, the kiss a sloppy mess. The orgasm was amazing. The kiss nearly as good.

I have no idea how men usually act after they cum, but I think it might be a good sign that I did all right since his tongue is in my mouth, his hand still wrapped between my legs.

"Arabella," he rasps low and deep.

I look up at him, my brow furrowing. Something isn't right.

But he kisses me again, his finger slowly withdrawing from inside my body.

And then he wraps his arms around me, pulling me up the bed and settling me into the cradle of his arms.

I sigh, snuggling deep into his embrace.

I have no idea how one-night stands usually go. Is snuggling usually part of the equation?

Part of me thinks I should offer to leave.

But part of me is ridiculously comfortable.

His muscular body has wrapped mine in a cocoon of warmth and security.

"That was amazing," I sigh out, my eyes closing.

"It was," he chuckles against my ear. "You were."

I grin, already in that place between wakefulness and sleep. "I'm pretty sure if one of us was the catalyst of the quality, that was you."

He chuckles low and soft. "Sleep, luv. You must be exhausted."

I do. I fall asleep in the warmth of his embrace.

But I wake a little while later, my sleep-addled mind aware that I'm alone in the bed.

The bathroom light is still on, and I hear Gris's lilting voice say two words…

"It's done."

Want to keep reading? King of Deception *is available on Amazon!*

STALK ME LIKE AN ALPHA!

Join my newsletter to get all the latest updates!

Tammy's Newsletter

And follow me everywhere else for teasers, giveaway, book news and fun!

www.authortammyandresen.com
www.facebook.com/authortammyandresen
www.instagram.com/tammyandresen
https://www.tiktok.com/@lordsoflasvegas
www://amazon.com/authortammyandresen

MORE ABOUT TAMMY

Tammy is the writer of Bestselling Regency Romance who could not resist the urge of writing in the dark and delicious world of Contemporary Dark and Steamy Billionaire Romance.

She lives with her husband and three children in Massachusetts and her favorite adventures are the ones that are found in books but occasionally she lives a few of her own!

Made in the USA
Coppell, TX
03 June 2026